The
Doomsday
Canyon

The Doomsday Canyon

Ray Hogan

G.K.HALL &CO.

Boston, Massachusetts

1985

Published in Large Print by arrangement with
Doubleday & Company, Inc.

British Commonwealth rights courtesy of Scott Meredith
Literary Agency

G.K. Hall Large Print Book Series

Set in 18 pt English Times

Library of Congress Cataloging in Publication Data

Hogan, Ray, 1908—
  The Doomsday Canyon.

  (G.K. Hall large print book series)
  1. Large type books. I. Title.
[PS3558.O3473D62 1985]   813'.54   85-5817
ISBN 0-8161-3836-2 (lg. print)

to . . .
the Henline siblings—Star, Bill, Robert
and Jewel—and all whom they hold
dear . . .

The Doomsday Canyon

1

John Rye kneed the big chestnut gelding he was riding in close to a jutting shoulder of rock and squinted into the midmorning glare. His hard mouth tightened as the three outlaws he was pursuing moved into view a short distance ahead on the narrow trail.

A surge of anger, of pure hate, raced through him. Jake Tolbert was one of the trio—the last in the line hurrying up the unstable, gravelly path. Reaching down quickly Rye drew the rifle hanging in its boot from the saddle and in a single, efficient motion levered a cartridge into its chamber, brought the weapon to his shoulder, and lined the sights on Tolbert's broad back.

The lawman held the long gun steady for several moments, finger lightly touching its honed trigger. It would take but the slightest pressure to send the heavy slug hurtling through the warm air and send the outlaw straight to hell where he belonged.

But it couldn't be. He must put personal feelings aside and do as he had been ordered: bring Jake Tolbert in alive.

Slowly, reluctantly, John Rye lowered his rifle, and then a moment later the outlaws—Tolbert, Bone Enright, and a youngster known only as Gillespie—had rounded a bend and were lost to sight. Rye swore grimly and releasing the hammer of his rifle, slid the weapon back into its boot. As if sensing the moment of violence was past, the chestnut, unbidden, resumed his course up the winding, rocky path.

Rye drew a bandanna from his hip pocket and mopped at the sweat on his hard-planed face. It was warm for early summer in the Arizona hills—but not that warm, he realized. It was the thought of Jake Tolbert that had sent fever raging through him—and that wasn't good. No lawman should ever permit personal feelings to influence either his judgment or his responsibilities; the law wanted Jake Tolbert alive for hanging; they

2

intended to make an example of him for other outlaws, show that no matter how clever, how callous, or how bold a man might be he could not flout the law and get away with it. Knowing outlaws as he did, Rye had doubts as to the effectiveness of the idea, but that was the way they wanted it and that's how it would be.

Rye had been up in Montana where he had been sent at the request of that territory's governor to track down and bring to justice a trader who had organized a band of renegade whites, dressed them as Indians, and terrorized the Sapphire Mountain area, robbing, burning, and killing, for several months.

The lawman had succeeded, although it had not been a case of bringing the trader in alive, and was preparing to leave for Denver, in the fledgling state of Colorado which he considered more or less his headquarters at that time, when word came directing him to report to Prescott, Arizona Territory.

He hadn't been aware that Jake Tolbert was to be the object of his attention until he reached that territory's capital. He had heard of Tolbert occasionally in the past couple of years but never anything specific—only that he was an outlaw of the more vicious kind, one ever ready to use his weapon at the slightest need or provocation.

This had surprised John Rye. When he had known Tolbert back in Dodge City the man was a gambler, one well thought of in the profession, and something of a dandy. It was said that Jake hailed from St. Louis and was the son of prominent, well-to-do parents who had disowned him.

Rye had felt a glow of satisfaction when the Arizona governor had told him the names of the outlaws he was to track down and bring in. Two of the three were of little consequence to him personally, but Jake Tolbert was something else. Of all the lawbreakers he had ever set out to capture, Tolbert was the one he would take the most pleasure in making his prisoner, while hoping all the time the man would make a desperate effort to escape and so produce the excuse for Rye to use his gun.

He had to forget that, Rye knew. As a lawman, one with a far-reaching reputation not only for fearlessness and a firm hand bordering on harshness when it came to dealing with outlaws: he was also considered utterly reliable and could be depended upon to follow explicit orders when—and that was seldom—they were given him. This was one

4

of those rare times. Ordinarily Marshal John Rye was permitted to do as his judgment dictated when trailing and capturing a wanted criminal, but this was different.

Jake Tolbert, together with Bone Enright and a third renegade named Gillespie, had hung around the Arizona capital for several days getting matters sized up. Then at an opportune time they had walked into the Rancher's & Miner's Bank, bulging on that morning with payroll money, and relieved the institution of fifty thousand dollars in new gold double eagles only recently received from the mint in San Francisco.

In the process Tolbert had needlessly killed two men and a woman and pistol-whipped a bank clerk so badly that when Rye rode out of Prescott some days later, after the outlaws who were reportedly holed up in the hills, the clerk had not yet regained consciousness, and there was small hope of his ever doing so.

Enright and Gillespie had not stood idly by while their partner was senselessly using his gun; they, too, took a hand in the slaughter, and when the trio rode out of town they left behind a total of five citizens dead, and three critically wounded.

The trail was cold when John Rye got on it. Posses organized by Prescott lawmen had already done what they could but had failed to locate the outlaws. However, they did determine that Tolbert and his partners were last seen heading into the Skull Valley country west of Prescott.

Rye chose to begin his search there where, the leader of the posse had told him, the outlaws had simply vanished despite the ring of deputies that had encircled the area.

John Rye was no believer in the ability of three men to simply vanish. They had to be somewhere, and working on that theory he eventually turned up a drifting cowhand who had noticed three riders, one on a black horse, one on a gray, and a third on a large bay, riding west from the Granite Basin country. The description of the horses matched that given to the marshal by the Prescott sheriff, and at once Rye, having nothing else to go on, followed out the lead. It was a different area, far removed from Skull Valley where they were supposed to have gone, but the horses were a giveaway. The outlaws, it would appear, had made a show of going to Skull Valley; instead they had circled back, passed Prescott on the north, and headed into the high mountains above it.

There Rye temporarily lost the trail, but

several days later he picked it up while talking to the owner of a small general store near Mingus Mountain. From him he learned of three men who were living in a cabin somewhere on the west slope of the eight-thousand-foot formation. Strangers to him, the merchant said they had stopped by to lay in a stock of supplies while on their way to do some prospecting.

No one did any prospecting on Mingus Mountain, the storekeeper realized, but the fact was only of passing interest to him. He was simply grateful for the new business and hoped for more.

His description of the horses again fit those being ridden by Tolbert and his friends; that of the men themselves meant little to the lawman. He hadn't seen Tolbert in years, the same applied to Bone Enright, and Gillespie was a stranger to him. But Rye was convinced the three purported miners were the men he sought, and getting directions from the storekeeper the lawman struck out for the west slope of the towering formation.

On the third day Rye spotted smoke halfway up the mountain, and working his way carefully along a fairly good if steep trail, he eventually drew in sight of a cabin.

He could neither see nor hear anyone around and, moving in close, picketed his horse in a stand of dense brush some fifty feet or so from the weathered old structure, then began to close in.

He was only a dozen strides short of the hut when the outlaws unexpectedly rode into the clearing that fronted it. Rye had a quick glimpse of Jake Tolbert's once handsome face, now bloated and set to cruel lines, of the younger man who would be Gillespie, and the third outlaw, Bone Enright, who was also known as Charlie Englehart. Years back Enright had escaped across the Mexican border when Rye, after him for the crime of murder, had got too close. The marshal had been pulled off the case shortly after that and sent on another by his superiors who apparently considered it more important.

At a disadvantage because of the uncertain footing near the cabin, Rye had brought up his pistol in hopes of at least crippling Tolbert and Enright, but the outlaws had opened fire on him instantly with four guns—Gillespie being a man who favored a weapon on each hip—and the marshal was forced to drop back behind a mound of rocks and brush. He did get off two shots, but neither of them was effective.

The outlaws had turned and fled at that moment, and by the time Rye could get to his horse and give chase they were gone and lost to sight. But he now had a fresh trail, and after making certain that Tolbert and his partners did not intend to return to their hideout, he set out in pursuit.

Now, on the second day after the encounter he was close—close enough to have shot all three of them out of their saddles, and that was exactly what he would have done could he have had his way. But the law wanted them alive, particularly Jake Tolbert, and he could do nothing but comply, regardless of the deep hatred he had for the gambler turned outlaw.

2

Jake Tolbert twisted about in his saddle and threw a glance back down the trail. John Rye was still there coming steadily on. Jake swore deeply, feelingly. He wished it was some lawman other than Rye dogging them. And then the outlaw shrugged as a hard smile pulled at the corners of his mouth; he'd beat John Rye once, and he reckoned he could do it again.

Brushing at the sweat glistening on his face with the back of a hand Tolbert eased the muscles in his aching back by shifting his weight from the left to the right stirrup. The dry smell of dust was in his nostrils, and the dull click of the horses' iron shoes striking rocks in the trail filled his ears. He was last in line as he and his partners made their way up the mountain they were crossing— something he'd not let happen again. Bone could bring up the tail end the next time, or let the kid, Gillespie; he'd eaten all the dirt he was going to.

Reaching back, Tolbert dug into the pocket of the left saddlebag, pushing aside the bag containing his share of the double eagles so he might get his fingers on the bottle of whiskey he was carrying. It was rotgut, and his nose curled as he put the neck of the container to his mouth and had a swallow.

Soon now, he thought as he lowered the bottle, it would be nothing but good bourbon for him; no more of this cheap saloon swill. With the money he had now he could start living right again—high on the hog, as some would say.

Twenty thousand dollars in gold—that had been his share. Back in the shack where they had hid out while the law from Prescott was running itself ragged looking for them in all the wrong places, he, Bone, and the kid had taken the opportunity to split their take from the Prescott bank. Fifty thousand didn't divide into three equal parts so he had played a hand of draw poker with Gillespie and Enright—winner to get twenty thousand, losers to halve the remaining thirty thousand. Winning had been easy. He'd never sat in a game with worse poker players, and when it was over they were still on a fairly friendly basis—not that Tolbert gave a damn one way or another.

Involuntarily Tolbert again turned and looked back. John Rye, like a threatening shadow, was a hunched shape on the big chestnut horse he was riding as he pressed stubbornly on. The lawman had looked about the same as he did a couple of years back when, unnoticed at a corner table in a small saloon, Jake had watched him stride into the place and collar an owlhoot he'd been trailing.

Rye had looked even taller than his six foot height then, and he still carried himself in that arrow-straight, shoulders-back, cocksure way of his. His hair was dark as ever, his brows still thick and overhanging as if to shield his eyes which were piercing and cold blue as always. He was wearing a beard that day probably because he hadn't had a chance to shave, and his mustache, full and drooping, appeared ragged.

Tolbert's mouth curled as he recalled the

incident. The marshal had looked all solid will and determination, especially in the dark clothing he was wearing, and when the owlhoot had made a gesture of resistance by reaching for the weapon on his hip, Rye had proven that the impression of hardcase toughness he gave was for real; he had whipped out the forty-five he carried and with the speed Tolbert had to admit was blinding, buffaloed the owlhoot alongside the head with it.

The man had been a damned fool to try and buck John Rye; Tolbert had to admit that also. The very looks of the lawman —grim-faced, icy cool, and with that superior, ruthless air about him—were enough to serve warning on anyone that he was not to be trifled with. The trick was for a man on the run to never let John Rye catch up with him.

But that, Tolbert also had to concede, was easier said than done. The lawman, who carried a special U.S. marshal's commission issued by the President, had the authority to go anywhere in the country after a fugitive and had the reputation of never giving up until the party he was pursuing had been brought to hand.

Abruptly Gillespie, in the lead, pulled his

horse to a stop. Enright drew in sharply to keep the gray he was riding from crowding into the hindquarters of the younger man's bay. Tolbert, cursing, pulled up short.

"What the hell's the matter with you?" Enright demanded.

Gillespie spat and pointed back down the trail at the distant figure of Rye. "What the devil are we running like scared rabbits for? There's only one of him and there's three of us!"

Bone Enright slid a glance at Tolbert. A lean, light-haired, brown-eyed man dressed in stained gray pants, dirty white shirt, scarred leather vest, run-over boots, and wilted-brim black hat, Enright looked to be—and was—a man long down on his luck. Brushing at his mouth with the tag corner of the red bandanna he wore about his neck, he shook his head.

"Why?" he asked in a controlled, patient voice. "You want to know why? It's because that ain't no two-bit, ordinary lawman dogging our tracks. That's John Rye!"

"So?" Gillespie said indifferently.

"That mean you ain't never heard of him?"

"Nope. I come from up Oregon way. Grew up there, in fact. I don't recollect ever—"

14

"Guess that explains your ignorance," Enright said, nodding. "Most everybody around here knows first hand or has heard of John Rye. Lots of folks call him the Doomsday Marshal."

"Doomsday Marshal!" Gillespie echoed. "What the hell kind of a handle is that?"

"You're likely to find that out now," Jake Tolbert said quietly.

"That's for dang sure," Enright agreed. "They call him that because once he takes out after a man he don't ever give up till he's collared him or put him under."

Gillespie, a husky, muscular man somewhere in his early twenties, with a thick shock of cottonlike hair, small dark eyes, a loose mouth, and clad in ordinary cowhand clothing, gave that thought. After a few moments he stirred.

"Sounds like this here Rye is a real genuine stem-winder."

There was a trace of derision in Gillespie's tone as if he didn't take much stock in what Enright and Jake Tolbert had said, but was inclined to humor the two older men.

"You ever have him tracking you, Bone?" he asked.

"Once," Enright replied, pulling his sack of tobacco and packet of brown papers from

15

a shirt pocket and rolling a cigarette. "Was four, maybe five years ago. Was after me for gunning down a deputy up in Nebraska."

"Can see he didn't nail you," Gillespie observed pointedly, a note of triumph in his voice. "That sure proves to me he ain't all that good—like you're claiming."

"Weren't no fault of his that I got away," Bone said, cupping a hand about a lighted match and touching it to the tip of the cigarette dangling from a corner of his mouth. "Was a couple of Texas Rangers —real green ones—got in between me and him. They figured they had more authority than Rye and wasn't about to let him do any lawing in their territory. While they was getting it all ironed out, I skedaddled across the border into Mexico."

Enright paused, took a deep drag on his cigarette, and expelled a small cloud of smoke. "Laid low there for two years—two lousy damn years of sweating it out punching cattle on a Mex *rancho!*"

Tolbert looked again at Rye. The lawman was still well in the distance, but coming on. Tolbert came back around, reached for his bottle, and had another comforting swig of the fiery liquor. Overhead several vultures were circling lazily, their attention on something in a canyon off to the right. A deer or some other animal, Tolbert supposed, or perhaps a man. In wild country like they were in, many things could go wrong.

"Don't sound much like Rye," he said then, shrugging. "Never heard of the border stopping him before."

"Not certain just what happened after I got across the line and hid out in a little 'dobe town. Was a lawman—another U.S. marshal—come hunting for me. I guess they must've sent Rye off after somebody they figured was more important'n me. Sure didn't make me mad. I mighty quick shook that tin star who took his place and headed on down to Chihuahua. Got myself that job I was telling you about on a *rancho* a ways below it."

The vultures were dropping lower, their circling had become tighter, Tolbert noted. A slight tremor passed through him. He'd seen a man, a corpse, once that the big, broad-winged scavenger birds had gotten to. It was a sight he'd never forget.

"How about you, Jake?" he heard Gillespie say. "This here old he-bear of a lawdog ever get after you?"

"Never gave him the chance," Tolbert

17

snapped. And then he added impatiently, "We're wasting time sitting here jawing. We're fools to let Rye get any closer to us than he is right now."

"Amen to that," Enright declared, flipping away the dead cigarette and scrubbing at his bearded chin. "We was lucky back there at that shack—being all ready to pull out anyway when we spotted him. Cost us our bedrolls but I figure that was a mighty cheap price to pay for getting away from him."

Gillespie hawked and spat into the dust in a show of disgust. "I'm thinking you both've got this here Doomsday Marshal jasper stacked up too high in your head," he said, raking the bay lightly with spurs and starting him moving forward again. "You being here right now goes to prove that this Rye ain't all you're cracking him up to be. If he was, old Bone there'd either be busting rocks—or dead."

Enright shrugged. Tolbert smiled in a tight sort of way. Gillespie was young; a man couldn't tell him anything. Too bad. His kind never lived long enough to wise up about life.

Maybe he'd been guilty of the same kind of arrogance, Tolbert thought. If he'd stayed with gambling, most likely he'd not be out here now in this godforsaken wilderness hurrying to keep out of reach of a lawman who, he knew, hated outlaws with an unholy passion and would kill if given only half a reason. But he'd not listened either to his own better judgment or to the advice of others; he had just gone right ahead doing what he wanted to—which hadn't worked out anyway—and ended up putting himself on the wrong side of the law.

"Hell—I ain't running no farther!" Gillespie announced suddenly. "I'm going to find me a place somewheres along here, take my rifle, and set that sonofabitch's sun once and for good. Maybe you gents are scared to do something about him, but I sure'n hell ain't!"

Enright glanced back at Tolbert and smiled resignedly. "I reckon you got a right to try," Enright said, "but you hold off till me and Jake gets past you before you do."

"Try—hell!" Gillespie shouted, swinging his horse in behind a bulge of rock and dropping from the saddle. Sweat shining on his face, he jerked his rifle from the boot, levered a cartridge into its chamber, and, waiting for his two partners to move on by,

19

leaned up against the rock and raised his weapon.

"Want you both watching this," he said. "I'm plumb tired of running from this bird and tired of listening to you bleating about him. I aim for you to see it when I knock him off that saddle he's forking."

Neither Tolbert nor Bone Enright made any comment, but both wheeled their horses about and, remaining mounted, put their attention on the steadily approaching figure of John Rye coming up the trail.

"When he gets to that there bend where that tree overhangs—I figure it'll be time to put a bullet in him," Gillespie said, pointing to a place on the slope where a ragged piñon tree hung down over the trail.

"That's a far piece," Enright murmured doubtfully.

"Not for me and old Betsy here," Gillespie countered, patting the rifle. Steadying himself he took aim at the oncoming lawman.

In the stillness that followed a squirrel scolded from a nearby pine, and a rustling in the brush crowding the shoulder of the trail indicated the presence of some other animal disturbed by the horses and their riders.

"Right now," Gillespie said softly. "Just

say goodbye to your Doomsday Marshal friend.''

The mountainside and nearby canyons echoed with the blast of the rifle. Rye threw up his arms and tumbled from the saddle. Gillespie laughed, and as the smoke from the long gun drifted lazily away he turned to his partners.

''What did I tell you? A bullet will stop a lawdog same as it will any man!''

Tolbert's narrowed eyes were on the big chestnut horse standing quietly on the path well below. He could not see Rye, the lawman being hidden by the base of the rock shoulder where he had fallen.

''He's off his horse for damn sure!'' Enright admitted admiringly. ''I got to tell you—that was one hell of a good shot! Ain't that so, Jake?''

Tolbert nodded slightly. ''You going down there and see if he's dead?''

''No need,'' Gillespie replied confidently, climbing back into his saddle. ''He's dead—or he's dying. Don't fret none about him no more.''

Neither Enright nor Tolbert made any comment, and the latter, cutting his horse about, headed on up the trail.

3

Rye, letting the chestnut have his way along the trail, kept his eyes fixed on the three distant riders. Wary at all times under such circumstances, the lawman was alert for an ambush, for any change—three riders abruptly becoming two or the complete disappearance of all from his view.

He'd experienced and weathered, only all too often, the tricks that outlaws desperate to throw him off their tracks tried and so was ready for most anything. Luck was with him in this particular situation; the trail, while meandering, was narrow and followed a fairly good grade as it ascended the mountain slope, thus enabling him to keep the outlaws in sight almost every minute.

Abruptly they were lost to him. Rye gave it little thought. The bends and occasional jutting boulders were not uncommon. More than likely they had simply rounded a sharp curve, one partly blocked by a shoulder of rock, and would shortly reappear. But true to the inherent caution that governed his life he took nothing for granted and began a sharper surveillance of the trail.

The chestnut plodded on, climbing steadily. After a short distance John Rye slowed the gelding's already laggard pace. The outlaws had not reappeared. Pulling to a halt beneath a piñon that overhung the path, the lawman studied the slope lifting before him.

Abruptly he drew up in the saddle. The hard, bright glint of sunlight striking metal had caught his eye. Ambush! The outlaws had come to a stop, and one of them was lining up a rifle on him. Instantly the marshal rocked to one side, the motion a fragment of time ahead of the long, echoing report of the gun.

He felt the heat of the bullet as it sped across his right shoulder, the pain preceding the weapon's report by the merest fraction of a second. Throwing up his arms in a gesture of pain Rye went out of the saddle to the ground. Then, as the chestnut shied off a few steps, the lawman allowed his body to settle in closer to the side of the trail so that the bulge in the slope would block him from sight of the outlaws and prevent him from becoming the target for a second bullet.

He was not hurt. The rifle bullet had raced across his shoulder doing little more damage than scorching his skin and tearing the fabric of his shirt. He hoped however, that he had made it appear to the outlaw marksman and his partners that he had been hit, had perhaps sustained a mortal wound. No doubt all three would be coming shortly to verify the fact.

Rye was hopeful of that also—and he would be ready. Keeping near the slight ledge at the foot of the slope Rye turned slightly to one side, reached into his shirt, and drew forth the hunting knife that he carried in a sheath slung below his armpit. Tucking the keen blade under his belt, Rye then pulled the forty-five from its holster and, keeping it in his hand beneath his body, stretched out on the loose dirt and gravel to await the arrival of the outlaws.

The minutes began to drag by. Insects buzzed angrily about his head. Two scrub jays flew into the ragged piñon, perched briefly, and then began to dart frantically about in the tree's sparse foliage. Nearby, the chestnut stirred restlessly, lowered his head, and began to graze on the thin weed and grass growth at the edge of the path.

Where the hell was Tolbert and the others?

Motionless, sweat clothing his body, Rye wondered which one of the outlaws it had been who fired the shot at him. Whoever, the man was an excellent marksman; it had only been the glint of sunlight on the rifle's metal signaling a warning that had destroyed his aim. Rye swore softly. Had he not seen the reflection the bullet would have caught him in the chest or perhaps the neck—and that would have been the end of it.

Was it Jake Tolbert who peered down the barrel of the weapon and centered the sights on him? Likely, Rye decided, but of course it could have been one of the others; it just seemed to the lawman that, judging from what had taken place in the past, it logically would be Tolbert who'd be the most interested in seeing him dead.

Rye hoped it would be Jake who came to have a look, for Tolbert was the one he, personally, wanted most. Sure, the law had ordered him to bring in Gillespie and Bone

Enright for their part in the Prescott killings, too, but it was Tolbert their grim interest centered on. Tolbert, it had turned out, had a long string of brutal murders to his credit.

He'd find it hard not to use his gun on Tolbert; he'd have to keep reminding himself that the law was holding him responsible for delivering the outlaw alive to the sheriff in the Arizona capital, where he was to be made an example of—but accomplishing that would be difficult, particularly if Jake Tolbert made an attempt to escape.

Rye stirred uncomfortably at the thought. Reaching up he swiped at the sweat misting his eyes and shook his head. He had no choice but to let the law have its way with Tolbert. Vengeance only begot vengeance, he had often pointed out; it applied to him also.

No man should take the law into his own hands regardless of the reason for doing so, just as the hatred and pain that had resulted from the act could not be counted as grounds for retribution. And he, above all—a trusted lawman—should not be considering such a course. His sworn duty was to bring in Jake Tolbert: afterward he could take his satisfaction from seeing the outlaw swing from a gallows in some prison yard.

He guessed now that it would be better if

it wasn't Tolbert who showed himself first on the trail, better if instead it was Bone Enright or Gillespie who came to make certain of his death. He could kill either of them with a clear conscience if they stepped in to put a final bullet into his head. But Tolbert—

John Rye shifted on the hard, gravelly surface of the trail. Ten minutes had passed—perhaps more. Time enough for the outlaws to have dropped back and had their look at him. Frowning, the lawman, flat on his belly, wormed his way slowly away from the slope, toward the center of the trail. Reaching there, hat off, he raised his head slightly and studied the bend in the trail where the outlaws had halted.

There was no one there—nor could he see any signs of riders on the trail in between there and where he lay.

The lawman cursed softly. So confident had they been of his death, or that he was mortally wounded, that they had ridden on. Rye guessed he'd made it look too good when he feigned being hit and knocked from his saddle. Too, they could have taken into consideration the time that would have been lost by doubling back down the mountain to have their look at him—figuring it only wise to hurry on into New Mexico and reach Texas, if that was where they were heading.

Drawing himself to his feet, the lawman recovered his flat crowned hat and studied the trail lifting gradually before him. The incident had cost him a good half hour, and in that time Tolbert and the others should have lengthened their lead considerably, particularly if the trail topped out a few miles farther on and their horses were favored with a down grade.

It didn't matter. He'd still run down Tolbert and his partners; this would only delay matters a bit longer. Turning to the chestnut the lawman—hunting knife back in its sheath and gun holstered—swung up into the saddle.

Again he put his attention on the trail, eyes narrowed to cut down the glare. The corners of his jaw tightened. A rider appeared briefly on the distant skyline, was silhouetted darkly as he topped out the grade, and started a descent on the opposite side. A second rider followed and then a third. The outlaws.

Rye shrugged. They had increased the distance that separated him from them, but not as much as he expected. Reaching into his shirt pocket he took out a leather case and removed one of the slender, black stogies that he often enjoyed. Thrusting the weed into his mouth, he returned the case to its customary place, procured a match, and, firing it with a thumbnail, held it to the cigar's end and puffed the slim cylinder into life.

That done, John Rye exhaled a cloud of smoke into the warm, still air, settled his hat forward over his eyes, and started the chestnut up the trail.

Tolbert and his partners carefully avoided all settlements those next few days as they bore steadily east, Rye noted. Not once did they pass through any of the few towns, and if they developed a need for trail supplies, there was no indication that they did anything other than go without.

All of which raised a question in the marshal's mind; since the outlaws were taking such care to not be seen, could that mean they were aware that he was not dead but was again on their trail? Or were they simply keeping out of sight on the chance that their presence might be noticed and reported to some local lawman?

The latter seemed more likely to Rye. He doubted they had caught a glimpse of him, as he was now well behind them in thickly wooded country that did not offer any lengthy views. Nor had he, at any time, caught sight of them.

Also, they were not avoiding the trail that cut its course through the mountains—only the towns and ranches were being ignored. Further, Rye regularly came upon the sites of their night camps, finding them always just a short distance off the trail.

It was impossible to make up lost ground to any extent, the lawman found, because of the mountainous country. But he was satisfied to simply hold his own, knowing that eventually the outlaws would break out onto kinder land where visibility would improve and his horse, a large, powerful animal, would cut down the lead the outlaws' lesser mounts had managed to build up.

There was also a good chance that Tolbert and his friends, weary of the trail, would finally halt in the first town of size, now that they were far enough from Prescott to have no fear of immediate danger.

Rye endeavored to recall what he knew of the country, bring to mind just what towns there were in the area. The trail, as far as he knew, led onto New Mexico, and the first settlement of consequence could be one in that territory.

The answer to the question came late on the fifth day after leaving Mingus Mountain when, having topped out a long, gradual rising, Rye found himself looking down upon a scatter of lights.

The lawman hurried on, feeling a flow of welcome warmness after so many long, empty miles of solitude. He wondered what the name of the settlement might be and if he was still in Arizona or had crossed over into New Mexico. That answer too, came, a short time later after his initial look at the town when he reached the first outlying structures.

A weathered sign on a fence post bore the name SHOW LOW. Rye brushed his hat to the back of his head. He knew where he was now. He had reached the town that had taken its name from a famed game of chance wherein a premises had changed ownership on the turn of a card—the settlement subsequently taking its name from the incident. And he was still in Arizona.

Chances were good that Jake Tolbert, Gillespie, and Bone Enright had stopped over to wager a bit of their wealth at Show Low's gambling tables and celebrate the success of their venture and escape. Rye hoped so. It had been a long ride from Prescott.

Turning into the narrow street along which the few houses and other structures were irregularly scattered, the lawman began a slow tour, his eyes searching each hitchrack that he drew abreast of for the outlaws' horses—a gray, a black, and a bay.

Midway through, a hard grin of satisfaction cracked the marshal's tight lips. At a rack alongside what appeared to be the largest and most active saloon in town were several horses. At its far end were the animals he was looking for.

Swinging up to the hitchrack and halting at a point opposite from where the outlaws' mounts were picketed, Rye swung off his saddle. Wrapping the chestnut's reins about the crossbar, he took a moment to check the pistol riding on his hip and, finding it ready, started for the entrance to the saloon.

4

Jake Tolbert, sitting at a back table with Enright and Gillespie, glanced about the haze-filled, odorous room that was Show Low's main saloon. Dusty, dirty, poorly lit by two wagon-wheel chandeliers, half the lamps on each of which were not burnng for lack of oil, the rest with weak flames struggling to break through cloudy, smoky globes; a bar crudely constructed of unvarnished planks and two-by-six timbers, with a back bar consisting of a shelf upon which were two dozen or so bottles of whiskey that were being reflected in a small, oval mirror that probably once saw service on a piece of furniture in someone's home.

Tolbert's lips tightened in disdain. Hell, a few years back he'd not have let himself be caught dead in a dump such as this! In those days he worked and drank in only the high-class houses, the best saloons, and, occasionally when the urge came to him, the riverboats.

He'd been a man of consequence then, one whom others respected and women fawned over. He had taken care to always look his best, stay clean, wear fine broadcloth suits, linen shirts, and expensive boots along with costly but tasteful jewelry. His hats were imported from London and delivered to him by a St. Louis clothier—all of which lent credence to his reputation as an honest gambler. He—

Tolbert shrugged as if to dismiss thoughts of the past, took up the glass of whiskey he'd been idly twirling between thumb and forefinger, and downed a swallow of the raw liquor. Involuntarily he made a face. Bone Enright, sitting across from him, laughed.

"Sort of like drinking coal oil, ain't it?"

"Worse," Tolbert grunted.

Again the outlaw allowed his dark, sullen eyes to drift about the room and over the dozen or so patrons present, some at the makeshift bar, others slumped in chairs or sitting at tables; at the like number of gaudily dressed women moving about talking, laughing, going about the business of soliciting customers for entertaining in one of the back rooms.

"I don't aim to even look at a place like this once I get back to the river," he said, more to himself than to his partners.

"Goes for me, too," Gillespie agreed, overhearing, half turning his chair to face one of the women advancing toward him. "It's Texas for me, and when I get there I'm going to be in tall clover!" he added and extended his hand to the girl.

Slim, dark eyed, she showed traces of having once been something of a beauty, but now the lines in her face and the dullness in her glance and fixed smile belied that.

"You buying me a drink, cowboy?" she asked, dropping onto his lap.

"You bet your boots I am!" Gillespie replied. "You got a place where we can go do some drinking?"

The girl nodded. "In the back . . . Just you grab us a bottle from Bender there at the bar and follow me."

As she came to her feet Tolbert laid his flat, dour attention on Gillespie. "We're damn near broke—don't be forgetting that."

Gillespie, rising, grinned broadly. "Oh, sure we are! Just about flat busted!"

Tolbert's expression did not change. "I mean that," he snarled. "You foul things up and I'll kill you!"

Gillespie sobered. "Aw, hell, Jake, I won't do nothing like that—and you know it. I got enough change to pay for what I'm aiming to buy without cashing any of them you-know-whats," he added, grinning at the woman.

Across the room a fiddler had struck up a tune, and several couples were gravitating toward the small square in a corner reserved for dancing. Gillespie grasped the girl's hand and turned to leave.

"See you jaybirds later!" he said as they hurried away.

Tolbert and Enright watched the pair circle by the bar, pick up a bottle of liquor, and then head for a door at the rear of the building.

"You figure we can trust him?"

Eyes partly closed, features set to impassive, almost cruel, lines, Tolbert shook his head. "Not sure, but if he crosses us—uses some of those double eagles—he's a dead man."

Enright stirred. "That won't help us none

if it brings the law down on us for that robbing and killing we done in Prescott.''

''Doubt if word's got down this far yet—and nobody knows we come from that direction—''

''Nobody but that damned marshal —Rye.''

Tolbert drained the last of the whiskey from his glass. ''You think he's still alive?'' he asked, frowning. ''I saw him fall off his horse with my own eyes.''

''So did I,'' Enright agreed, ''but knowing him, I wouldn't take no bets on it. Only time I'll ever feel for damn certain he's dead is when I see them put him in a hole in the ground and start shoveling dirt in his face.''

Tolbert gave that thought while he refilled his glass from the bottle on the table. Another of the saloon women sidled up, looking first at Jake Tolbert. Turned away by the hostility in his manner, she put her smile on Bone Enright.

''You want some company, honey?''

Enright shook his head. ''Maybe later.''

''Suit yourself. My name's Emma. I'll be here somewhere.''

Bone came back around, readjusted the pair of saddlebags draped across his legs, and faced Tolbert.

"How much money we got? Enough to make it to Texas?" Enright raised his voice slightly, just enough to be heard above the stomping on the dance floor.

"I don't know what you've got—"

"I'm down to a couple of dollars," Bone replied.

"About what I've got."

Enright muttered under his breath, then: "The kid'll be busted time that woman gets through with him. No use figuring on any help from him. Now, we're needing grub. You reckon spending one of them double eagles would be too risky?"

Tolbert nodded. "Best we take no chances. Might get by, but it would be our luck some lawman'd turn up and, hearing about three men spending new gold, get on our trail right quick—and it's still a long ways to Texas. Anyway, I'm not sure if I saw telegraph wires coming into this town or not when we rode in. If there is, the law here will know about the bank in Prescott."

"I didn't see no wires either," Enright said, finishing off his drink. "Maybe we ought to go outside, look around. Might find the telegraph office if they have one and we can't spot the wires. Then we'd know for sure—"

Tolbert brushed the idea aside with a wave of his hand. "No, we play it safe. We go poking around out there in the dark we'll draw the law real quick. We'll just sit around here a bit, rest up, then move on. We'll get some money and some grub somewhere down the line."

Bone Enright smiled, indicated his understanding. Refilling his glass from the now near empty bottle, he again adjusted the saddlebags, heavy with his share of the gold coins and other personal items, hanging across his knees and settled back.

"What're you aiming to do, Jake, when we get to Texas?" he asked.

Tolbert was quiet for a long minute, then: "Never been much of a hand to look ahead very far. Like as not I'll keep on going —maybe till I get to St. Louis. With the stake I've got, I can get back to card playing right away—with the high rollers on the riverboats. Or I might even open up a place of my own."

"Saloon?"

"Yeh, the whole thing. Can probably buy out somebody, fix up the place real fancy so as to draw the big spenders. Could run the casino myself, hire a bartender and the rest of the help I'd need."

"Women?"

"Seems you've got to have them," Tolbert said. "They do draw customers. You got any plans?"

Bone Enright took a swallow of whiskey. "Sort of like you, I ain't long on making plans—man just can't be sure of ever getting to carry them out. But I'd kind of like to get in the horse-raising business. Buy me a little spread somewheres, one where there's a lot of good grass and water, stock it with some Morgans—"

"You know horses that good?"

"Well, yeh, guess you can say I do. Worked for a jasper before the war who raised them, then during the war they put me in charge of the stables of the outfit I was with. Got to know how to handle the critters real well."

"Sounds like the right thing for you to do, assuming you get the chance to do your choosings—that we all do, in fact."

Enright swore gloomily. "I savvy what you mean. I could wind up in Mexico again."

"We all could. A lot depends on us getting to Texas without drawing any attention. We make it to there, the place is big enough for us to easy lose ourselves."

"And changing our names—that'll make it better."

Both men glanced up as Gillespie, face flushed and happy, came up to the table. Reaching down he took his saddlebags off his chair, hung them over a shoulder as Tolbert was doing, and sat down.

"You got any money?" Enright greeted.

Gillespie grinned more broadly. "Sure, fifteen thousand dollars. You needing a loan?"

"Cut out that kind of talk!" Tolbert snapped. "Somebody might be listening."

The grin died on the younger man's lips as he wagged his head. "No, I sure ain't got no money. That little gal cleaned me slicker'n hog fat. I'm plumb busted. Why, we needing cash?"

"We're needing grub, that's what we're needing," Enright stated. "Enough to get us across New Mexico into Texas—and we can't use none of that gold," he added lowering his voice, "if we aim to get there."

"Sure is funny," Gillespie muttered, rubbing at his jaw. "We're all stinking rich but we ain't got the cash to buy a few dollars' worth of trail grub."

"Don't get all worked up about it," Tolbert said indifferently. "We'll get by. Big

41

thing is to forget about what we've got in these saddlebags until we get to Texas. Then you can do what you damn please with your share.''

"I've got mighty big plans for that!" Gillespie said. "Real big plans. First off I'm going to buy me a—''

The younger man's voice broke, his features knotting into a frown of disbelief as he came slowly upright. Both Tolbert and Bone Enright also came to their feet, the latter with mouth agape and eyes opened wide.

"It's him—by God!" Enright said in a strangled sort of voice. "I knew he wasn't dead—just plain knew it.''

Gillespie had stepped away from the table, now squarely faced the doorway of the saloon, and the poised figure just within its entrance.

"Maybe he ain't—but he damn sure will be now!" he shouted and made a stab for his guns.

5

The door was open allowing a rectangle of yellow light to spill out on the landing that fronted the saloon. Again pausing briefly, this time to let his eyes adjust, Rye moved through the entrance and came to a halt a step inside the noisy, haze-filled room.

There was a good crowd—perhaps a couple of dozen or so—on hand, the majority of whom were paying customers. A fiddler was the sole source of the music for two parties stomping out a clog in the area set aside for dancing, and a card game was going on at one of the several tables that were scattered about. No one was at the bar at that moment, the remaining patrons inside the odorous room being sprawled indifferently in the chairs spaced about the tables.

The night's usual business had not yet begun, Rye suspected. It would be an hour or more before the men working the ranches and lumber camps drifted in—and for that the lawman was grateful: the fewer persons around, the fewer he had to contend with.

Rye saw Tolbert and his partners at that moment. All three were at a table near the back of the room. Shoulders to a wall, they were but a half-dozen steps to a door that evidently let out onto the area behind the building. It was far from an ideal situation in which to confront the outlaws, Rye thought, but then there seldom was a good time. Men knowing they faced the gallows, or even a term behind the high stone walls of some penitentiary, almost always chose to fight their way out or die trying, rather than surrender.

Hand hovering close to the pistol on his hip Rye started slowly toward the rear of the saloon. He was hoping to get as many of the patrons off to one side and out of the line of fire which he was certain would erupt. His movements, the set look on his chiseled, inscrutable face, the flinty promise of violence that his very appearance evoked when he again drew to a halt brought a sudden hush to the saloon.

The silence immediately caught the wary attention of the outlaws. The younger man came abruptly to his feet, an expression of amazement blanking his features. Tolbert and Enright also lunged upright, knocking their chairs over as they stepped back. In the next breathless moment Gillespie yelled something and went for the pistols on his hips.

Rye drew and fired, the motion a fluid blur. The outlaw, both weapons up, staggered as the lawman's bullet smashed into him. He rocked again as a second slug halted the continuing rise of the pistols clutched in his hands. He hung motionless for a fraction of time and then began to sink slowly to the littered floor.

Rye, wisps of powder smoke hanging about him, swung his attention immediately to Tolbert and Enright. Both men, each now with a screaming, protesting woman clamped to him as a shield, were backing hurriedly toward the door in the rear of the saloon. Gun up and ready, the lawman started for them, glancing to either side as he did as if assessing the probability of interference from sympathetic onlookers.

No one appeared to have such in mind, and he rushed on, crossing the distance from where he stood, just within the saloon's entrance, to its rear in long purposeful strides, all the while seeking an opening to use his weapon and wound the outlaws before they could escape.

But the opportunity never came. Tolbert was the first to reach the exit. With the frantically struggling woman still held in front of him, he holstered the pistol he had drawn, opened the door, and plunged out into the dark night, still holding to his human shield. Enright, following a like procedure, was only a step or two at his heels.

Rye quickened his stride and conscious now of a rising mutter and murmuring behind and about him, gained the closed door. Standing a bit to one side so as not to present himself as a target silhouetted in the opening to the outlaws no doubt waiting for him, he yanked the heavy panel open.

Immediately the two distraught and disheveled women, half prone in the opening where the outlaws had discarded them, sought to regain their footing. Passage momentarily blocked, Rye knocked the pair roughly aside and rushed on out onto the hardpack at the rear of the saloon. He came to a halt, the sound of horses racing away into the night coming to him from the direction of the hitchrack.

Cursing, Rye wheeled, ran back through the doorway of the saloon. By cutting through the building he could save steps and time—perhaps get a shot at Tolbert and Enright as they rode off.

Another curse ripped from the lawman's mouth. The two saloon women, shaken and dazed, were just inside the opening. Several of their sisters in kind, along with the bartender and a half-dozen men, were clustered about them, offering consolation.

Rye, grim with anger as he realized Jake Tolbert and Bone Enright were again escaping, shouldered his way roughly through the gathering and ran for the entrance to the saloon.

"Hold it right there, mister!"

Rye continued on, aware of the speaker, a man off to one side, aware of Gillespie's sprawled shape beside the chair where he had been sitting, and aware of the threatening hush that filled the room.

The deafening blast of a gunshot and the splintering of the floor a step ahead of Rye brought him to a stop. Pale eyes bright with fury, mouth a hard, straight line, he spun to face the interruption—a tall, young man in dark clothing wearing a town marshal's star.

"Who the hell you think you are—coming in here, shooting down a man, going after his friends?" the lawman demanded. Gun leveled, he moved in closer. "I'll take that iron of your'n. Now drop it on the floor."

Rye studied the younger man coldly. He shook his head. "I'm not about to. And you best holster that pistol of yours before you get hurt," he said quietly.

The town marshal, startled by the warning, frowned. He made no reply for several moments and then recovering his composure, gestured with his weapon.

"Don't go threatening me. I'm the law in this town and—"

"And while you're standing there blocking my way, two outlaws wanted back in Prescott for murder and robbery are getting away," Rye cut in sharply.

"A goddamn bounty hunter!" a voice in the crowd exclaimed. "Went and shot down that young fellow like it was nothing, Luke! I say we take him out and string him up!"

"Ain't nobody hanging nobody around here unless the circuit judge says so," the marshal stated flatly. "And don't none of you go getting ideas t'otherwise."

"It's what he's got coming," another man standing at the bar insisted. "You best be taking care of the likes of him, Luke, or the town's going to be overrun by them."

"I'll see to the lawing around here," Luke replied evenly and addressed his words to Rye. "That right—you a bounty hunter?"

Rye shook his head in disgust. Tolbert and Enright were well on their way and out of reach of even a bullet by then. There was nothing he could do now but get the young, thickheaded lawman off his back and when morning came, try to find the trail of the fleeing outlaws and head out after them again.

"No, I'm a special U.S. marshal. I've been tracking these three killers—the two you let get away and the dead one there on the floor—for days." Rye's tone was cold as Montana norther.

Luke swallowed hard and glanced around. Then, as if gathering courage, he said: "You got a name? You got something that'll prove who you are?"

"I'm John Rye," the federal lawman replied crisply. "Put that gun away and I'll get my papers out and show you. I'm not about to reach into my inside pocket with you standing there pointing that forty-five at me.''

Luke thought that over briefly and then again looking about as if seeking con-firmation for what he was going to do, lowered his weapon.

''All right. Let's see them papers.''

Rye took the leather folder containing, among other items, the special U.S. marshal commission issued by the President from its place inside his shirt. Handing the document over to the town's lawman, he crossed to where Gillespie lay. Reaching down he picked up the outlaw's saddlebags and hung them across his shoulder.

''Reckon he's telling us for true,'' he heard Luke say to the crowd in general.

At that a man standing close by nodded vigorously. ''Sure, I recollect seeing him now! Was thinking he looked familiar. He's the one they call the Doomsday Marshal 'cause he usually shoots first and then—'' The speaker broke off abruptly as if fearing to say more. ''Seen him over Santa Fe way a couple of years or so back,'' he finished, lamely.

Luke had carefully folded the presidential authorization and was holding it out to Rye. The marshal accepted it in silence, returned it to the leather billfold and thrust the packet back into his shirt. That done, he passed the outlaw's saddlebags to the young lawman.

"Want you to take care of this. Probably around fifteen thousand dollars or so in new double eagles in them, if the bunch split what they took from that bank in Prescott. Have the bank here handle the return. I'll need a receipt so—"

"Can't do that, Marshal," Luke broke in with a shake of his head. "We ain't got no bank, and I sure ain't got no place that'd be safe to keep it."

Rye shrugged wearily, slung the pouches over his shoulder. He would simply have to hang onto the money until he reached a town where the gold could be deposited safely.

"Expect you can take care of him," he said, pointing at Gillespie. "His horse and gear's out at the hitchrack. Can sell them to pay whatever the cost comes to."

"Sure, I can do that, all right," Luke answered. "I'm mighty sorry I caused you to let them others get away, but there weren't no way I could know you was a U.S. marshal. What did you say they had done?"

"Held up a bank in Prescott. Killed several people, shot up a bunch more that'll likely die. Got away with fifty thousand in brand new double eagles that had just been delivered by the San Francisco mint.''

Luke whistled softly while those of the crowd within earshot exchanged glances. ''Can sure see why you're so fired up—''

''The law in Prescott wants them bad —Tolbert and Enright, their names are. Killings they did were all unnecessary—just did it for the hell of it.''

Luke wagged his head as murmurs ran through the saloon. ''I'm saying again I'm right sorry, Marshal,'' the young lawman said, repeating his apology. ''Come morning I'll get a posse together and help you pick up the trail.''

''I seen two riders headed out on the trail to Springerville when I rode in a bit ago,'' a man standing at the bar volunteered. ''That who you're talking about?''

Rye turned to the speaker. ''Could be. Did you get a look at their horses?''

''Not close. One was dark—maybe a black or a bay. Other'n was either a white or a gray.''

Rye nodded his satisfaction. That would be Bone Enright and Jake Tolbert. ''Them, all right,'' he said. ''How far is it to Springerville?''

''Forty, fifty mile, more or less—''

Forty, maybe fifty miles. Rye brushed at the stubble on his chin. He was tired and hungry, felt drained. No doubt the same applied to the chestnut gelding after the long hard days in the mountains with only grass for feed.

"There a place around here where I can put up for a few hours?" Rye asked.

Luke said, "Sure can use my place—house out back of the jail. Ain't much but you'll be comfortable . . . You ain't figuring to light out after them two right away?"

"No, morning will be soon enough—they won't get away from me . . . Where can I get something to eat?"

"Only place is next door—"

"And my horse. There a stable where he can get a graining and some rest?"

"I'll take care of that myself, Marshal," Luke said. "You go on, get yourself supper. I'll drop back by in a bit, and if you're done eating, I'll show you to my shack."

Rye nodded his appreciation and with Gillespie's saddlebags over his shoulder, turned to the saloon's front door. He could sure use a good meal—and a mattress bed was going to feel mighty fine. But he'd allow himself to enjoy such comforts for only a few hours; it wouldn't be wise to wait too long in getting on the Springerville road after Tolbert and Enright.

6

Despite John Rye's determination to rest only briefly and get an early start, it was near first light when he awoke. The restaurant next door to the saloon was not yet open, and contenting himself with a cup of black coffee made for him by one of the saloon girls, he went to the stable, got his horse, and rode out for Springerville immediately, saying little to anyone.

A light rain had begun to fall, one not so hard as to require his putting on the Mexican poncho he carried for such occasions, but it did lower the temperature in the high, mountain country through which he was passing. Consequently it was a relief when the sun rose, the rain ceased, and a warmness spread across the land.

That Jake Tolbert and Bone Enright were ahead of him on their way to Springerville was unquestionable, but at the first opportunity—a place where a small creek crossed the road and created a muddy sink—Rye dismounted and, examining the soft edges of the swale, found the signs of two horses coming in from the west and emerging on the east side.

The tracks were somewhat washed out by the early morning shower, but in the lawman's mind there was no doubt the prints had been made by the horses of the men he was after. He need only to continue, checking the trail whenever he could to be certain Tolbert and Enright were still in front of him and had not swung off onto a course across open country.

That, the marshal figured, was unlikely. The rugged, wild mountainous area to either side of the established route appeared far too broken and difficult for a man on horseback to venture into.

He wasn't too fearful of an ambush, doubting that Tolbert and Enright would spend the necessary time; they apparently were anxious to reach Texas where they expected to find sanctuary, or perhaps their intentions were to go on into Mexico—which they could easily do once they were out of Arizona Territory and in New Mexico Territory.

To head south now for the border would take them into hostile Indian country; but by riding on until they reached the Rio Grande they could follow the river to the border where they could cross over with no problem other than dodging any American soldiers or Mexican *federales* who might at the time be keeping an eye out for anyone endeavoring to ford the wide, muddy stream.

Rye drew out one of his stogies, lit it, and settled deeper into the saddle. It was pleasant riding through the remote hill country. There were no ranches, no homesteads, no settlements—only long graceful slopes, grass covered at times, rock studded at other, scrub brush, patches of colorful wild flowers, and tall pines the tops of which swayed gracefully in the light breeze as if fanning the bright blue sky above them.

Gray doves were plentiful, as were songbirds, and Rye saw several pairs of quail that had forsaken their home coveys and were setting out to build nests and start families of their own.

Around midday Rye halted at a small stream for lunch and to give the chestnut a bit of rest. There had been no mercantile store open in Show Low where he could restock his supply of trail grub—now down to a few strips of jerky, a hard biscuit or two, and a handful of coffee beans.

Searching through the saddlebags of the outlaw Gillespie, the lawman failed to turn up anything edible, finding only a few articles of clothing, some extra pistol cartridges, and his share of the gold stolen in Prescott. Rye had not bothered to tally the amount, but he assumed the outlaws had split the fifty thousand three ways. It would be a big relief to turn the cash over to the law in Springerville when he got there or to a bank if there was one available.

Rye had no way of knowing how near he was to that settlement, and when darkness had closed in and he could see no signs of a town anywhere in the distance, he pulled in for a night camp. He could find little need to press on under the circumstances. Better to keep himself in a top, honed condition and be at his best when he caught up with the outlaws—which he was certain to do.

One thing that had improved were the odds; where it had been three to one, they had lowered with the death of Gillespie —likely the best hand of the three men with a pistol. Not that being on the short end of the odds was anything new to John Rye; in truth, that was the usual way of it, and he'd long ago adjusted his mind to the fact that the law always seemed to be at a disadvantage and played out his hand accordingly.

He built no fire, substituting a good swallow of whiskey from the bottle he had in his saddlebags for coffee. No doubt Tolbert and Enright had reached Springerville by that hour, even if they had halted along the trail after leaving Show Low that previous night. It didn't matter. He was only a few miles behind them, and despite the probability of their not staying over in the settlement but pushing on, he'd still eventually overtake them. Jake Tolbert was one outlaw he'd spend the rest of his life pursuing if necessary.

The glowing salmon flare of sunrise found Rye again on the trail that continued to follow a due east course. There had been another light shower during the night and all things had a freshness—the leaves and needles of the trees, the clumps of brush, the grass, even the lowly weeds seemed to sparkle in the first slanting rays of the sun.

He couldn't be far from Springerville, Rye figured. The settlement had been only forty, or maybe it was fifty miles from Show Low to begin with, and while traveling through the mountainous country had been slow, the lawman still reckoned he had covered a good two-thirds of the distance. He supposed he could have ridden on and covered the remaining few miles the previous night, but he was not regretting his decision to halt. Both he and the chestnut had benefited from the rest and would be in much better condition when they reached the settlement and—

Rye pulled to a stop, the sound of voices coming to him from beyond a bend immediately ahead. It wouldn't be Tolbert or Enright, he knew; was likely a party of pilgrims enroute to Show Low or some other town farther west. Moving off to the side where the sun was not in his eyes, the lawman folded his arms across his chest and, slack in the saddle, waited for the travelers to appear.

They proved to be a man and a girl. He was a rough-looking individual with small, mean eyes and a scraggly beard. He was dressed in faded army-issue clothing and wore a battered kepi on his head. Riding double behind him on his bay horse was a girl of seventeen or so. Pretty, with blond hair, she stared at the marshal in silence.

"Howdy, friend," the man greeted. "I'm Anson Smith. This here's my daughter Euly."

Rye nodded, quoted his own name.

"Seen you coming from a rise back a ways, figured you might be acquainted with these parts—"

The lawman shook his head. "Stranger, myself."

Smith clawed at his beard. The girl Euly continued to stare, and Rye had a feeling that she was frightened of something but dismissed it, thinking she was probably just tired from her place in back of the saddle.

"Well, seeing as how you was coming from the west I reckon you know how far it is to this here town they call Show Low."

Rye started to reply and then clamped his mouth shut. A noise in the brush behind him sent tags of warning racing up his spine. The lawman turned his head slightly, swore silently. He'd fallen for one of the oldest tricks in the game. A second man—red hair, pale-eyed, slovenly dressed, like Anson Smith—was standing in the road grinning broadly, a leveled pistol in his hand.

7

"That there's my partner, Rube—Rube Henry," Rye heard Smith say. "Now, he's kind of trigger-happy so you best do just what he tells you to."

The lawman shifted his attention to Smith. The man had also drawn a pistol, had it cocked and leveled at him. The girl still maintained her frozen stare, and one of her wrists, visible to the marshal now, bore red chafe marks as if it had only recently been bound too tight with a cord of some kind.

"Throw down your gun—right here in front of me," Henry ordered. "And be dang sure you do it careful-like."

In the tense hush that followed Henry's

command, Rye slowly pulled his weapon from its holster and tossed it to the ground.

"We're sure mighty obliged to you for coming along, mister," Anson Smith said in a whining way. "We're needing a horse right bad. The nag Henry was on stepped in a dog hole and busted a leg. Had to shoot the critter.

"When that happened, Rube had to start riding the animal we'd sort of borrowed back a piece for the gal here and she had to climb up behind me. We've got a long ways to go—California—and she ain't been looking forward to setting there back of me for all that ways."

"Thought you were headed for Show Low," Rye said, watching Rube Henry narrowly.

The lawman cared nothing about the destination of the two saddle tramps, was simply making conversation in hopes of keeping Anson Smith occupied while he sought the opportunity to jump Henry and gain the upper hand.

"Just talk while old Rube there got hisself around in back of you. But I expect we'll be pulling up there anyway, unless you got some grub in them saddlebags. We run mighty low on fixings. Me and Rube didn't figure on feeding three when we lit out. Picking up the little gal was kind of unexpected.''

Henry, bending over, retrieved Rye's forty-five, thrust it under the waistband of his stained, baggy trousers, and stepped back.

''You're packing two pairs of saddlebags —what's in them anyway?'' Smith asked, shifting to a more comfortable position on his horse. He still had his weapon pointed at the marshal, but Rube Henry had thrust his back into the scarred holster that hung slightly forward on his hip.

''Sure carrying a lot of something,'' Henry said.

Stepping up to the chestnut the outlaw unbuckled one of the pockets, probed its contents briefly, and then drew back in surprise—a muslin bag of clinking coins in his hand.

''Lord a'mighty!'' he breathed in a raspy voice. ''We're rich! This here sack's full of double eagles—brand new ones!''

''What?'' Smith's eyes were wide as he stared at his partner. ''You sure them are real?''

Henry let several of the coins he was holding in his hand spill back into the bag.

"You're goddam right I'm sure! You think I don't know a double eagle when I see one?"

Smith, as if in a trance, wagged his head disbelievingly. "Ain't that. I just can't figure us having such good luck," he said and turned his attention to Rye. "What are you a'doing with all that gold, mister? You own yourself a bank?"

"I'm a U.S. marshal," the lawman replied coldly. "That gold belongs to a bank in Prescott. I—"

"Prescott!" Henry echoed. "Hell, you're heading the wrong direction if you're going to Prescott. Now, I'm betting you stole it from that there bank and you're legging it for Texas or maybe Mexico."

Rye swore under his breath. Gold was always trouble. He should have forced the lawman in Show Low to take it off his hands, make up a posse, and return it to Prescott.

"Well, whatever," Anson Smith drawled, "we'll take care of it from here on—don't you fret none about that."

"And I'm mighty obliged to you, too, for this horse," Henry said, returning the gold to its place in the saddlebag and buckling the strap securely. "It's sure going to pleasure me a heap to be riding a fine animal like him. Now, just you climb down so's I can take over."

Rye, taut as a coiled spring, dismounted slowly and stepped back. If he were to act, it would have to be soon, but the threat of Smith's cocked and leveled pistol nullified all ideas that came to mind. It wasn't all over with yet, however.

"Come on over here, gal, and get my horse. You'll be riding him," Henry said.

The outlaw reached for the chestnut's reins as the girl, Euly—probably Eula, the lawman thought—slipped from the back of the bay Anson Smith was on. At once the chestnut began to shy and swing about.

"Good luck," Rye said dryly to Rube Henry. The big gelding just could be the means for turning the tables on the two drifters.

Henry paused, stared at the lawman. "What the hell does that mean?"

"That horse of mine's not much for making friends. Could say he's a one-man horse. Anybody but me tries to mount him he acts up—and if somebody does make it into the saddle, he starts pitching."

Rube spat in disgust. "I ain't never seen the nag I couldn't ride," he declared. "Don't expect I've come across one now."

Rye cast a hurried, sidelong glance at Anson Smith. The outlaw still had his weapon leveled and ready but his attention was now divided—partly on Rube and partly on him, the marshal saw.

"Been thinking about all that gold," Smith said, unexpectedly. "How much you figure's there, Rube?"

Henry, struggling to get the nervous chestnut settled down so that he could mount, swore loudly. "Hell, I don't know! Never took no time to count it. Must be ten maybe fifteen thousand dollars."

"Whooeee!" Smith murmured. "He right, mister? There that much in that bag?"

Rye, standing with arms folded across his chest, nodded. His right hand had slipped inside his shirt. His fingers had wrapped themselves about the hilt of the knife carried in a sheath below his armpit. The blade was his last hope.

"Maybe more," the lawman said.

Smith laughed in a high, almost hysterical way. "This here thing gets better and better! Come on, Rube, let's get going. Sooner we reach California, sooner we can start enjoying all them double eagles." The outlaw paused, watched his partner shorten up the chestnut's reins as he struggled to control the gelding. "What'll we do with the gal? Sure don't have to bother with her now."

"I don't give a goddamn what you do with her!" Henry shouted in exasperation as he attempted to slide a foot into the stirrup of the chestnut's saddle. "Leave her here with this jasper or take her along for company at night—all the same to me!"

"What are we doing with him?" Smith asked as if the question had just occurred to him. "Can't leave him here either. Liable to talk—"

"You got a gun in your hand, ain't you?" Henry demanded as the chestnut continued to shy. "Use it. Put a bullet in his head —which sure'n hell is what I'm about to do with this contrary broomtail—"

The chestnut pivoted wildly, half dragging Henry, one foot in a stirrup, with him. The big horse was suddenly in between Rye and Anson Smith. Henry, clinging to the saddle horn with one hand, the other entwined in the chestnut's thick mane, was immediately in front of the lawman. John Rye reacted instantly. Knife tight in his fingers, he drew and struck. There was a flash of sunlight on the bright steel as it arced toward Rube Henry, a gasp of pain from the outlaw as the sharp blade drove deep into his body.

As Rube began to fall, Rye released his grip on the knife. He caught the outlaw around the waist with his left arm, jerked the pistol from the man's waistband, and with the chestnut gelding still between him and Anson Smith, he snapped a shot at the outlaw.

The bullet caught Smith in the chest, rocked him back in his saddle. And then, as the girl's scream added to the echoes of the pistol's blast, the weapon fell from the outlaw's nerveless grasp, and, toppling forward, the man went to the ground.

Instantly the girl, eyes wide, rushed toward the marshal. "Oh—thank you! Thank you—thank you!" she cried, her voice filled with relief.

Rye, flashing a wondering glance at the girl, relaxed his hold on Henry's lifeless body and allowed it to fall. The motion disturbed the chestnut; which began to pull away but halted when Rye checked him with a firm grip on the reins.

"You can't imagine what it has been like—being with those—those two men!" the girl said, her voice calming somewhat.

Rye only barely heard as he was crossing to where Anson Smith lay. The man was dead, of that the marshal was certain, but at such times it was never prudent to take it for granted. Kicking the outlaw's pistol off into the brush Rye felt for a pulse, verified what he believed. Rising and coming about, he faced the girl, the words she had just spoken now registering on his mind.

"Smith said you were his daughter." She was older than she'd appeared at first, the lawman realized. Probably around twenty.

She met his hard, questioning eyes squarely with a shake of her head. "No, sir—that's not true. He lied, told you that just to be talking while Rube circled around behind you. My name's Pearl Joplin. Friends and folks call me Pearly."

Rye, doubling back to where Rube Henry lay, recovered his knife and returned it to its concealing sheath. Flipping open the loading gate of his own forty-five, he rodded out the spent cartridge and replaced it with a fresh one.

"How'd you happen to be with them?" he asked.

"They grabbed me—kidnapped me. The part about stealing a horse for me and then Rube's animal breaking its leg is true—but that's the only truth they told you."

Rye considered her words and nodded.

70

Then: "Where you from?"

In his mind's eye he was seeing a problem taking shape; a young woman—probably far from home—suddenly on his hands. Having part of the stolen gold was bad enough, but that could be taken care of; a girl with him, one he'd have to be responsible for was something else! Her presence just might interfere with his overtaking Jake Tolbert and Bone Enright. Unconsciously the lawman swore softly; interfere maybe—but not prevent. He'd let nothing do that—not even a young woman desperately needing help.

"My folks live over in the western part of New Mexico—near a town called Milligan's Place. They have a homestead there."

"Where'd you run into these two?"

"I'd gone to Socorro—that's a town in New Mexico, too. Was going to visit some relatives—my aunt and grandmother. You know Socorro—about it, I mean?"

"Been there a couple of times, passing through."

"Well, I rode in with some neighbors of ours. They were hauling a load of lumber into Socorro to sell. They let me off near the church—my aunt lives in the south end of town so I was going to walk the rest of the

71

way. It was all to be a surprise to my grandmother and aunt, anyway, and I didn't want them to see me come up on a wagon-load of lumber. I wanted to just walk up and knock on the door.''

Rye, conscious of the minutes ticking away, each one of which would be separating him farther from Enright and Tolbert, turned, caught up the horse Rube Henry had been riding, and tying it to a close-by sapling, picked up the outlaw's body and hung it across the saddle.

''What are you going to do with them?'' Pearly asked, her story temporarily suspended.

''Turn them over to the law in Springerville,'' Rye answered, releasing the horse and leading it to where Anson Smith lay. Lifting the man's body, he placed it next that of Rube Henry, behind the saddle. Securing the two lifeless shapes so they could not slip off, he came back to the girl.

''Haven't said yet just how they come to grab you—''

Pearly appeared to resent the tone of voice in which the lawman put the question. She flushed slightly and then shrugged.

''They just rode right up to me while I was walking along the street—actually, it's more like a trail. Asked me if I could tell them where the sheriff's office was. I told them to go around to the plaza, and then the next thing I knew Rube had grabbed me, tied a rag around my mouth and some rawhide cord about my wrists, and was putting me up on Anson's horse. Anson took off real fast. It was all I could do to keep from falling off."

Rye rubbed at his jaw. "Nobody saw any of this happening? Seems in broad daylight—"

"Nobody," Pearly replied, coolly. "And it wasn't broad daylight—it was almost dark."

8

Rye studied Pearly Joplin thoughtfully. She was pretty, just as he had noted earlier, with brown eyes and light hair. Her nose was small and had a spray of freckles across it, while her cheeks were a healthy tan with a faint rosiness underlying the smooth skin. Her lips were nicely shaped but her chin had a firmness that seemed almost contradictory to the rest of her features.

Under a wool jacket, she was wearing a red-and-black-checked shirt—doubtless once the property of a man but made over to fit properly—a dark-blue skirt, and tan high-top shoes. A red scarf was around her neck while a brown, narrow-brimmed hat—again, the type generally worn by a man—with the crown pushed up to accommodate her hair, was on her head.

"I—I look a sight," the girl murmured, fussing with the front of the skirt when she became aware of his steady gaze. A frown crossed her features, one of revulsion when her glance strayed to the dead men. "It was terrible being the—the prisoner of those two for so long—"

Rye shifted his attention to the land beyond the trail. "Expect it was. I've been dealing with their kind for a good many years . . . You said your name was Pearly Joplin. Why was Smith calling you Euly?"

The girl's shoulders stirred. "That was his ma's name, he said. He liked it so he started calling me that."

"I see. Didn't you try to get away from them? Seems you must have had a chance somewhere along the way."

"They had my wrists tied together while we were riding. Then when we'd pull up to rest or eat or for night camp, they'd tie a rope around one of my limbs—my ankle —and sort of hobble me."

Pearly hesitated, trembling slightly at the remembrance. "Anyway, once we were a long way from town—from Socorro, what could I do even if I did get loose? We never did stop until near midnight, and if I had run off, how far could I have got on foot?"

"Not far I reckon—"

Pearly stiffened, and her eyes filled with an angry brightness. "If you're thinking I didn't want to get away from them, that I enjoyed their manhandling me—you're badly mistaken!"

"Not intending that," Rye said calmly.

"I grew up on a homestead—a nothing place far as life is concerned. Nothing but work! Milking cows, shearing sheep, cutting wood, cooking, mending clothes, cleaning and scrubbing, and a dozen other such things. I was ready to trade that kind of living for 'most anything, but certainly not for a life with those two animals. I tried my best to—"

"Never mind," Rye said, shaking his head. "I understand."

"Maybe you think you do, Marshal—if that's what you are. I don't think you believe me."

The lawman smiled. "Well, I am—and I do. Let it drop there. I'm going on to Springerville, turn these two over to the sheriff or whatever kind of law they have there, and then get on about my business.

Smith's horse is yours now. You can mount up and head out for any place you want, or you're welcome to ride with me. It's your choice—but I expect you ought to get word to your folks. They're probably worrying plenty about you."

"Maybe. Most likely don't even know what's happened. Neighbors I rode in with will have told them they let me off in Socorro, and since my grandma and aunt didn't know I was coming—it being a surprise visit, like I've said—my ma and pa won't even start wondering about me for a spell."

"It could be weeks then before they realized you are missing—"

"More like a couple of months. My folks didn't have much time for me. It was my brothers who counted, mostly because they were all big and strong and could do a man's work. I was expected to be just like them, and while I could keep up pretty good, there were some things I plain couldn't handle."

"You talk like you've had some schooling—"

"A little. There wasn't a regular school in Milligan's Place, but a man who worked at the general store had been a teacher back East somewhere, did some teaching at night after he got off work. There were about a half dozen of us that would go over to his place—a little shack behind the store—and he'd teach us how to read and write, and talk, do sums."

"Looks like the people in this Milligan's Place would fix up a room where he could hold a school—even pay the man a little for what he was doing."

"Not the folks around Milligan's! They don't set much store in book learning, as they call it. Having a strong back is what counts. I'm nineteen years old, save for a couple of months, and I've never known anything but hard work except for the times when I could slip off and go to Mr. Cleveland's teaching class."

Pearly's features softened and her eyes took on a dreamlike quality as she thought of the man who had taken time to impart bits of education to her and several others in Milligan's Place.

"One thing I have decided—I'm not going back home," she declared firmly as Rye crossed to the horse Anson Smith had been riding. "I've had enough of that—I'm going out on my own."

The lawman motioned for her to mount the horse she would be using. "Best I get on my way, but first the stirrups on your saddle will need shortening," he said. Then, when she had settled in the battered old hull, added: "Going out on your own—I don't know about that. It's not much of a world for a young woman by herself. Kind of work you'll have to—"

"I'm not figuring on finding myself a place in a saloon, if that's what you're worrying about. I guess I could get by playing cards—I watched Anson and Rube trying to beat each other at poker every night when we stopped for camp. They didn't have any money, just gambled for matches. Sat in the game myself after I got the hang of it."

"Doubt you'd ever make it as a gambler," Rye said, finished with the left stirrup and circling the horse to reach the right. "Lot of men try it but not many of them are good enough at it to make a go in the business. Besides—"

When Rye paused Pearly smiled down at him. "Besides men wouldn't like to play a woman gambler, that what you intended to say?"

The lawman nodded. "It's the truth. I've come across a few women running games but—"

"No matter," the girl broke in with a

shrug. "I don't plan on taking up cards as a way to make a living. I aim to find me a regular job somewhere—in a store maybe. And if I could get myself some more schooling, maybe I could become a teacher."

"That'd be the smart thing to do," Rye said, stepping back, the adjustment to the second stirrup finished.

He turned at once to the chestnut and taking up the reins, swung into the saddle, his movements hurried. He'd lost more time than he should, and it would be slow going with the two dead men hanging across a horse.

"You made up your mind what you're going to do now?" the lawman asked, gathering in the lines of the horse he would be leading. "If you go with me to Springerville, I'll want you to make other plans from there on."

Pearly nodded. "I see," she murmured as they moved onto the trail.

There was silence for a while, and then Rye glanced at the girl. "Coming up from Springerville, did you come across two men—one riding a black, the other a gray?"

Pearly shook her head. "No, we didn't. Fact is I never even saw Springerville—and neither did Anson. We circled it, and then

Rube went back and used what cash they had between them to buy grub. Why?"

"Outlaws I'm after were ahead of me. Thought you might have seen them. They probably got off the road when they heard you coming."

"They the ones who stole all that gold from the bank?"

"It, and a lot more," the marshal said. "Was fifty thousand dollars all together. They killed several people doing it."

"Sound like real bad ones—"

"They are—especially one called Tolbert," Rye replied, unaware that his voice had hardened and a stiffness had come over him.

Pearly considered him for a long breath. "Seems you have a special hate for that one—Tolbert."

He shrugged. "No use for any outlaw. Were three of them to start with. Had to kill one of them—Gillespie—back in Show Low."

Pearly was quiet again for a brief time. Then: "I've been wondering—what's it like to shoot a man—kill him, I mean? You never changed expression back there when you drove your knife into Rube and shot Anson."

Rye's chiseled face was inscrutable,

appeared to be made of stone. His narrowed eyes were colorless.

"Man with the kind of job I've got does what he has to do," he said in a voice that stated clearly the subject was closed, and then raking the chestnut with his spurs, he put the big gelding to a faster walk.

9

"Damned outfit ain't got nothing on the bar to eat," Bone Enright said, voice heavy with disgust. Climbing back into his saddle, he added, "First town I ever seen where the saloons ain't got free lunch for a man."

Jake Tolbert stared moodily off into Springerville's solitary, irregular street. It was just past sunrise, and the town was beginning to stir.

"Got to scare up something to eat somewhere," he muttered.

A tight, hard smile pulled at the corners of his mouth as the thought again occurred to him. There was over thirty thousand dollars between him and Bone Enright, and they dare not spend a dime of it—not unless they wanted to chance leaving a trail that might lead some lawmen to them and bring about their losing not only all of those bright, new double eagles, but most likely their lives as well. And hungry and whiskey-thirsty or not, Jake Tolbert was not risking that; he'd gone through too much hell to get his hands on the gold to risk losing everything.

Enright glanced back up the road along which they had entered the settlement. They had been careful to not be seen and so far felt certain they had left no trail for anyone to follow—except, maybe, that damned law-dog John Rye. They just weren't sure if he was still tracking them or not. Chances were better than good that he was.

"Can't hang around here for long," Enright said nervously. "Some jasper'll spot us for sure—and if that marshal shows up asking around, he'll find out real quick that—"

"Let him," Tolbert cut in irritably, reversing his thinking. "I'd like a chance at cutting him down. Getting mighty sick of running from him."

Enright frowned, scrubbed at the stubble on his chin while he studied his partner thoughtfully. "Sort of got the idea you was like me—plenty anxious to keep out of his way,'' he said after a time.

Tolbert shrugged, abruptly shifting his attention to a side road coming in to meet the town's main street. A rider had appeared —a small man riding a heavy-bodied farm horse and followed by a shaggy, black-and-white dog.

''Ain't nobody but some hayshaker,'' Enright said, noting Tolbert's quick interest. ''What're we going to do about some grub? Long ways yet to Texas.''

''Hunt us up a general store—one at the edge of town where we won't be bothered —and help ourselves,'' Tolbert replied.

Enright grinned, bobbed his head appreciatively. ''Now, that's a right good idea! Can grab all the grub we'll be needing, along with whatever the counterjumper's got in his cashbox. Where you reckon we can find a store setting out alone like you said?''

''Didn't see one on the way in, and we best pass up that one down the street. Let's circle the town and see if there isn't another one on the road out.''

Bone Enright made no reply but, raking his horse with spurs, led the way around the saloon he had just looked into, followed the alleyway that paralleled the street behind the buildings, and reached the opposite end of the settlement.

"Just what we're a-looking for!" he exclaimed, pointing to a fairly large, tin-roofed building on the opposite side of the roadway.

Tolbert only nodded. "Looks like they've got one customer," he said, as they crossed over and drew to a halt behind a shed. "Hold off until he's gone, then we'll move in and take over."

Enright twisted about on his saddle, raised a leg, and hooked it over the horn to relieve the aching of his back muscles. Brushing his hat to the back of his head, he rubbed at his jaw and looked off over the hills.

"Jake," he said in a tentative voice, "you reckon maybe this time you can leave off the shooting and killing? Back there at that bank, there just weren't no need to go—"

"You look out for your hide and I'll look out for mine," Tolbert cut in coldly.

"Sure—I'm for that, Jake, but—"

"What the hell difference it make now anyway?" Tolbert again broke in. "They can only hang a man once no matter how many scalps he's got tied to his gun belt."

"Yeh, maybe so, but cutting some jasper down just because he looks at you

86

slanchwise—"

"There goes the customer," Tolbert said, ignoring Enright's last words, and clucking softly to his horse, rode toward the store.

They pulled in behind the wood and metal structure and stopped. Tolbert sat for a few moments glancing about, getting his bearings, and deciding which route would offer the best possibilities for escape should anything go wrong and it became necessary to make a run for it. The road bearing east ran alongside the store's wagonyard, he saw. It led away from the town and into a good stand of pine trees and other growth; he and Enright could lose themselves quickly in the dense growth.

"What're we stalling for?" Bone wondered, impatiently.

Tolbert only shrugged, and maintaining his usual dour, close-mouthed manner, swung off the saddle. Tying the black to the crossbar of the hitchrack the merchant had provided, the outlaw walked slowly toward the steps leading up to the rear door of the establishment. Reaching the landing, he paused, waited for Bone Enright, and then, when his partner was beside him, crossed the small platform area, pulled open the door, and entered.

The interior of the store was small, considering the size of the building, indicating that the owner probably also maintained living quarters under its roof, but it appeared to be well stocked. The shelves were lined with canned goods, boxes, neatly folded articles of wearing apparel, kitchenware items, and other things of use to homesteaders and ranchers.

There was a glassed-in case containing pistols and knives, and in a rack behind it was a cabinet of rifles and shotguns. Placed about on the floor and arranged so as to create aisles were stacks of water buckets, washtubs, horse collars, saddle and harness racks, and similar articles of necessity.

The good aroma of cheese, of spice, and of freshly baked bread filled the place, and for a moment Tolbert remained motionless just within the door remembering bygone days when these were commonplace to him and not part of a time of violence.

"Something I can do for you gentlemen?" a voice called from behind a counter to the left. "Didn't see you come in."

Tolbert, Enright at his shoulder, walked deeper into the store. The merchant was an elderly man—white-haired, ruddy-faced, and with watery eyes aided by steel-rimmed spectacles. He wore a flowered calico shirt, nondescript trousers, and a clean, white bib apron.

"Riding through. Short on a few things," Tolbert said blandly, employing his best cultured manner. Although his formal education had not been extensive he more than made up for the lack by association with lettered men while working the riverboats on the Mississippi and the high-class gambling houses of St. Louis, New Orleans, Cincinnati, and like cities.

"Saw you were open and decided to do our stocking up. You run this place all by yourself?" the outlaw finished.

"Me and the missus," the storekeeper replied and half turned as a door back of him opened and a woman appeared.

Evidently the merchant's wife, she was about his age, had a lined face and gray-streaked brown hair, and wore a floor-length mother-hubbard dress with a lace collar.

"Got us some new customers," the storekeeper said. "They're just riding through and they want to supply up before they go on."

The woman smiled. "They're just in time for some of my light bread. Just took it out of the oven."

Tolbert's cordiality vanished as quickly and as easily as it had appeared. Jerking his head at Enright, he said, "Start collecting the things we need and putting them in a sack. I'll have a look at the cashbox."

The storekeeper frowned, not certain he had heard right. "Now, I'll get you whatever you want," he stammered as Enright, taking one of the folded sugar sacks placed on the counter, stepped up to the shelves and began to fill it with cans of tomatoes, beans, and peaches, packages of biscuits and coffee, and any other item that caught his eyes.

"They're here to rob us!" the woman cried, suddenly realizing what was taking place.

Tolbert drew his weapon and fired point-blank at her. The bullet caught her in the chest, set her dress to smoking, and drove her back against the wall and the shelving lining it. The impact jarred loose a dozen empty coal-oil cans, all of which came clattering down upon her lifeless, crumpled shape. Unnecessarily Tolbert sent another bullet into her body.

The storekeeper stood as if paralyzed, mouth agape, horror filling his eyes. And then wheeling, he seized a large butcher knife used for slicing cheese that lay on the counter and lunged at Tolbert.

"You—you murdering sonofabitch! I'll—"

He got no further. Tolbert raised his weapon again, fired. The slug drove into the storekeeper's belly. He rocked back, grabbed for the edge of the counter to keep from falling. Jake triggered another shot, sending this one into the man's heart and driving him to the floor.

With smoke curling about him, the outlaw calmly reloaded his weapon and then, thrusting it into its holster, crossed to one of the small windows that permitted a view of the street. There was no one in sight; the gunshots had not attracted the attention of anyone. Pivoting to face Enright who had been halted momentarily by the shooting but who now was again prowling the store for articles of food and other useful items, Tolbert moved toward the counter.

"You about ready?" he asked.

The calmness of the man was unnerving to Bone Enright. He nodded vigorously, and when he replied, his voice was unsteady. "Yeh—yeh, all done," he said and held up two large-size money belts. "Figured these would come in handy."

Tolbert only grunted his agreement as he

stepped in behind the counter and located the store's cashbox. It was locked. Picking up the butcher knife dropped by the merchant, he pried open the lid of the tin container and dumped its contents—an assortment of silver coins—onto the worn, wooden surface before him. Raking the money off into a palm and dropping it into a pocket, he looked at Enright, now waiting near the doorway.

"How much?" Enright wanted to know.

"Ten dollars or so," Tolbert replied in disgust. "A stinking ten dollars."

"More'n we got—that we can spend," Enright said with a grin.

"It'll get us to Texas," Tolbert said, "figuring the grub you've put in that sack. Sure you got all we'll need?"

"All I could think of," Enright answered. Then crossing to the door behind the counter, he added: "All 'cepting some of that fresh bread the old woman was talking about."

He disappeared into the room after stepping over the bodies of the storekeeper and his wife, returned shortly with two round loaves of still-warm light bread. Handing one to Tolbert, he continued on to the entrance through which they had come.

"Can make a meal on this while we're riding," he said. "It'll save us from pulling up till we're a far piece from here—something I figure we better be real soon."

10

The going was slow. The horse carrying the bodies of Rube Henry and Anson Smith, a thin, overworked, and poorly fed animal, had difficulty climbing the steep slopes and then, conversely, keeping its footing on the sharp downgrades. Several times Rye called a halt to rest and finally decided to unload the bodies and bury them alongside the road. But at that moment Pearly Joplin's voice stopped him.

"There's the town—"

Rye moved over to the slight rise where the girl stood and glanced ahead. Springerville was a small, close scatter of buildings lying in the near distance. A rueful smile split the lawman's mouth. It had taken almost the entire morning to travel what had been but a few miles to the settlement. But they were finally there, and within a very short time he'd be able to rid himself of the girl, the bank's gold, and the bodies of the two outlaws. Putting the horses into motion again, the lawman moved his party on.

Reaching the main street and paying no mind to the fifteen or twenty persons standing about conversing in small groups, Rye guided the horses toward a building that bore the sign JAIL over its door.

"Something's going on," Pearly said as they drew up to the hitchrack of the squat-looking structure. "Too many people just doing nothing but talking."

Rye nodded absently, his thoughts elsewhere. If Tolbert and Enright were in Springerville, they would know of his arrival by that moment—riding down the center of the street as he had—and either they'd pull stakes and hightail it again or they'd find a place to hide and watch for a chance to get him in their gunsights.

"What've you got there?"

Rye put his attention on the young man wearing a town marshal's star who came out of the combination jail and lawman's office.

Lean, with sharp, dark eyes and an intense manner, he regarded Rye suspiciously.

"I'm a federal marshal," Rye said. "Those two hanging across that horse kidnapped this young woman and later tried to rob and kill me. Who are you?"

"Ben Winters. You got a name and something that says you're who you claim you are?"

Rye dug into his pocket and produced his papers of identification. Several persons had drifted in from the groups gathered in the street, some pausing to have a closer look at the bodies of the outlaws, others moving in close to the lawmen in hopes of hearing what was being said.

Winters satisfied himself with Rye's papers, returned them, and offered his hand. "Pleased to know you, Marshal. You just happen to run into that pair or were you trailing them?"

"Run into them," Rye replied as the town's lawman crossed over to examine the dead outlaws. "One's called Rube Henry. Other one said he was Anson Smith. That's the names they gave the lady and me."

Winters frowned, nodded. "Looks sort of familiar to me, both of them," he said and turned to Pearly. "Where you from, miss?"

"New Mexico Territory. They grabbed me while I was in Socorro visiting. If it hadn't been for Marshal Rye, I'd been on my way yet to California with them. That's where they were taking me."

"Too bad. Sure hope it wasn't too hard on you."

"Enough," Pearly said and looked away.

"You got a bank here?" Rye asked, coming down off the chestnut.

"Sure don't—not a real one anyway. One of the general stores has a big safe. Lets folks use it. You needing to cash a draft or something?"

"Forget it," Rye said, dismissing the subject. He could see no need to let the word out that he was carrying a large amount of gold. "Like to turn these stiffs over to you for burying and ask you to look after the lady for me."

Winters frowned. "No problem with the first, ain't so sure about the second. What'll I do with her?"

"Can see that she gets back to New Mexico—"

"I'm not going back there—leastwise not back to my folks," Pearly cut in. "Told you that, Marshal. I want to keep riding with you."

"Considering what I'm up against, you know that's out of the question," Rye snapped impatiently, and as the girl dismounted, he turned to Winters. "Been tracking two killers. Men named Tolbert and Enright."

"What'd they do?"

"Held up a bank in Prescott. Was three of them at the start, had to shoot one back in Show Low. They killed several people, got away with a lot of gold—new double eagles. Was hoping I'd catch up with them here."

Winters' eyes were bleak. "Got a feeling you maybe just missed them," he said and jerked a thumb at the people scattered about on the street. "That's what all the hullabaloo's about."

Rye came to attention. "Meaning what?"

"Two men, we figure from the tracks we found out back of the place, robbed old man Radmon's store sometime early this morning. Killed him and his wife and took what money was in the cashbox. We found the Radmons about an hour ago. That sound like the pair you're after?"

"Could be. Tolbert rides a black horse, Enright a gray. If anybody saw—"

"Nobody seen anything—and we can't be too sure it's the tracks of their horses we found because there was some rain during the night. Prints were the only ones near the hitchrack, however—and the Radmons were alive early. Was a fellow, one of the local cowhands, in there right after the store opened and bought some tobacco.''

''Tolbert and Enright were headed this way—for Texas, I figure. How were those folks killed?''

''Shot—both of them twice. Was no need for two bullets. The Radmons had to be dead from the first one, coming from close range like it apparently was. We kind of got the idea the man who done it was enjoying what he was doing.''

John Rye's features had become stiff and cold and a hardness came over his eyes. ''That would be Tolbert,'' he murmured, half aloud.

''He one of them that likes to shoot a man?'' Winters asked.

Rye nodded. ''One of the worst.''

The young town marshal turned then to a group standing nearby. Motioning at the bodies of Rube Henry and Anson Smith, he said, ''Couple of you take this horse down to the livery stable and unload it. Tell Anse we'll be burying them two in potter's field—and pass the word I'll be mounting a posse to—"

"No—forget the posse," Rye interrupted. "Want you to leave Tolbert and Enright to me. I consider them mine. Too late to do any good with a posse, anyway. It would just get in my way."

Winters shrugged. "Whatever you say, Marshal. Been wondering—this Tolbert mean something special to you—more'n just being another outlaw? Kind of notice something change in you every time he's mentioned."

"Could be," Rye said and, wheeling, started for his horse.

The sooner he got on the trail after the killers, the better. They had a pretty fair start on him, despite the fact that he'd cut down their lead considerably; it would be smart to press on and close in on them now. But he was running short on trail grub, and since there was no way of knowing just where trailing the outlaws would take him, he'd best stock up while he had the opportunity.

"There another general store close by?" he asked of Winters.

The lawman pointed down the street. "Abe Goodman's. Can get most anything you want there."

Rye murmured a thanks and, turning on a

heel, took up the chestnut's reins and started for the store, a hundred feet or so away.

"What about me?"

The marshal became aware of Pearly Joplin's presence at his side immediately. He glanced at her.

"That's your choice. If you don't want to go home, maybe you can find yourself a job here in Springerville."

Pearly's expression changed. "I—I want to go with you," she said in a low voice.

The lawman slowed. "Can't let you do that. Men I'm going after would as soon shoot you down as they would me."

"That don't scare me—and I can shoot a rifle real good."

Rye smiled tightly. "Now that would be the quickest way I know of for you to get yourself killed—letting them see you coming toward them with a gun in your hands."

"That'd be all right with me, John—as long as I was with you."

Rye came to a full stop and faced the girl. "Not sure I savvy what you mean by that—but if it's what I think, forget it."

The lawman's voice was hard, but when he saw the crestfallen, stricken expression on Pearly Joplin's features, his manner softened and his tone relented.

"There's no place in my life for a woman. I found that out years ago. I'm gone all the time, never able to be home—and it's wrong to put a woman—wife in that position. Too—you deserve more from life than loneliness and worry."

"I wouldn't mind—and I could ride with you—"

"No, that wouldn't work out. I'm on the trail for weeks sometimes—maybe even for months, no matter what kind of weather —hot, cold, wet, or dry. Been out of grub now and then, and it's not often I get to sleep with a roof over my head."

"That wouldn't matter either. I've been with you some, seen how it is—"

"You've seen one day, and things haven't been the least tough. It's no life for a woman, and you're far too pretty to waste yourself on what a man like me could give you."

Rye resumed his course for Goodman's General Store—a small, narrow building with a steeply slanted tin roof and high windows.

"I think I'm the best judge of that," Pearly said stubbornly.

"You're wrong there," Rye replied, his voice again firm. "You don't know for sure about anything except for what went on back there in the town where you came from. Give yourself a chance, girl. Don't waste yourself on something that you'd likely turn out to be sorry for."

"I'd never be sorry being with you—being your wife or your woman. Can't we just give it a chance?"

They reached Goodman's and halted at the hitchrack. Securing the horses, Rye, after hanging Gillespie's saddlebags across his shoulder and with the girl at his side, entered the mercantile. It took only a quarter of an hour or so to fulfill his needs, and with his purchases in a flour sack he returned to his horse—Pearly Joplin staying close to him all the while.

"Don't you think we could just try—me going with you?" she suggested again as they freed the horses and started back up the street for the marshal's office.

Rye would have ridden out direct from Goodman's and wasted no more time in Springerville if he had not felt an obligation to see the girl safe, in good hands, before departing. That she found herself caring for him and wanting to become a part of his life was flattering, but it in no way fit in with the harsh, basic manner of living that was usual for him. There could never be another woman—wife—again under any circumstances; such a permanent commitment had ended once and for all time.

"Can't let you do it," Rye said as they drew near the marshal's office. "I'll make you a deal, however. You stay here and do some thinking. I'll be coming back through with Tolbert and Enright on the way to Prescott. We can talk it out then."

Pearly Joplin nodded woodenly. "All right. How long will you be gone?"

"Hard to say," the marshal replied. "Could be a couple of days—or it could be a couple of weeks—but I'll be back."

Halting at the hitchrack fronting the jail, Rye tied the flour sack to his saddle, slung Gillespie's leather pouches across its skirt, tied them down, and reached into his pocket for several coins which he handed to the girl. Then, as Winters came through the doorway of his office, Rye smiled and nodded to Pearly.

"Little cash to keep you going till I see you again," he said in a low voice.

"Got your grub sack all filled, I see," Winters observed cheerfully. The street had pretty well cleared of bystanders, most of whom could now be seen gathered at the livery stable. "Sure you don't want a posse to side you?"

"Obliged," Rye said, going up into the saddle. "This is a one-man job. You can do me a big favor though."

"Name it, Marshal—"

"See that the lady here gets a decent place to stay while I'm gone."

"Sure thing. The parson's got a room at his house. Can put up there. You're planning on coming back through, I take it."

Rye nodded. "Have to return my prisoners to Prescott for hanging."

"Good—just what they've got coming . . . I've been going through my wanted dodgers for them two jaspers you brought in. Haven't found them yet, but I'm sure I've seen them . . . Which way you heading out?"

"East. Only logical way for Tolbert and Enright to go."

"Expect you're right. Well, good luck, Marshal. Hope you catch them."

"I will," Rye said. And glancing down at Pearly, added, "Be looking for me soon."

She made no reply as he swung away on the big chestnut horse and pointed for the road that led out of town.

"That man's mighty sure of himself,"

Winters commented dryly, brushing his hat to the back of his head.

Pearly's eyes were fixed on the departing lawman. After a time she stirred. "If you ever saw him when he was in a tight and the odds were all against him, you'd understand why," she said quietly.

11

"This here bacon sure smells good," Bone Enright said, stirring the dozen or so strips of meat about in the skillet he was balancing over the fire. It was early morning, and the air, heavy and damp, kept the smoke hanging low.

"It about ready?" Tolbert demanded grumpily. "And what about those potatoes. Seems they—"

"You figure you can hurry up the cooking any you're sure welcome to try," Enright shot back. "Hell, I ain't no cook—never claimed to be—and I sure never signed on with this outfit to be one!"

Tolbert's laugh was a dry, humorless

107

sound. "You're doing fine, partner. Just ragging you a little." Then: "Expect we're both a bit touchy because we haven't had a square meal since we left Prescott."

Mollified, Bone Enright drew back from the fire. "Reckon the bacon's done," he said and motioned at the pair of tin plates he'd acquired at the general store they'd robbed in Springerville. "Cut open a couple of them potatoes and I'll pour some of this hot grease on them. Make them a mite tastier."

Tolbert did as directed, passing the plates on to Enright who added a portion of the sliced bacon to each, and then saturated the halved baked potatoes with drippings. While Enright was busy at that, Jake filled their cups, also taken from the Springerville merchant's stock, and divided the last of the light bread which was warming on a rock near the flames.

The two men fell silent as they ate their early meal, each working steadily at the process like people who had gone too long without food. Finally, when it was done, both settled back to sip their coffee—the brew sharpened considerably by liberal additions of whiskey to each cup.

"I reckon we sure fooled them people back in that town. Ain't seen hide nor hair of any posse." Enright said.

"We didn't leave a trail for them to follow," Tolbert pointed out.

Enright shrugged, shook his head. "Well, you damn sure give them plenty of reason to come after us. Weren't no need to shoot that storekeeper and his wife. Could've just batted them over the head—"

"And left them alive to talk, tell who it was that robbed them? The way it is now nobody can tie their killings to us."

" 'Cepting maybe John Rye. You forgetting him?"

"The hell with him—"

"Maybe so," Enright said doubtfully, refilling his cup, "but he ain't like any other lawman. Got a way of outguessing you and knowing what you'll be doing."

"You don't see him around anywhere, do you?" Tolbert asked caustically.

"Nope, but this here day's just starting. He didn't get that Doomsday Marshal name for nothing, and—"

"I know," Jake cut in impatiently, waving his partner to silence. "A lot of bragging going on about no man ever gets away from him. *You* did."

"I was mighty damn lucky," Enright said, "and I don't mind admitting it." He paused, lit one of the cigars he'd helped himself to back in the Springerville store. "I hear you say you knew him but that he never got on your trail for something?"

"Right," Jake replied, gently sloshing the last of the liquid about in his cup. "When I saw him back there at that cabin on the mountain, it was the first time I'd laid eyes on him in years."

Enright blew a small cloud of smoke into the morning air and watched it hang motionless for a time and then begin to slowly dissipate.

"There a beef of some kind between you two?"

"It's him that's got a beef against me—" Tolbert checked himself. "We've got company," he continued softly, allowing his hand to drop to the pistol on his hip.

Enright quickly swung his attention to the edge of the clearing behind him. Three Indian bucks, slumped on their ponies, were facing them stoically.

"Hell, them's friendlies," he said. "All they're looking for is something to eat. They won't give us no trouble."

Tolbert set his cup down and produced one of the cigars Enright had given him. "You're the bird that knows these redskins," he said indifferently. "Invite them in and let them clean up what's left."

Enright got to his feet, turned to the braves, made the customary motion for eating, and then beckoned them in. The Indians hesitated briefly and rode in, seemingly a bit fearful. Young bucks, they were thin, hollow-faced, and looked as if they could use a meal.

"Must've been a hard winter," Enright said, picking up the spider, and adding the last of the bread and potatoes to the bacon that remained in it. Nodding to the braves he offered it to them.

They came off their horses quickly. One seized the frying pan, drew off to one side, and squatted. At once the others hunched beside him, and shortly all three were digging greedily into the contents of the spider with their fingers. Finished, they set the pan by the fire, all the while smacking loudly. One turned to Tolbert and Enright.

"Whiskey? You got?"

Enright shook his head and pointed to the pot resting on the rocks over the fire. "Coffee."

The brave spat to show his disdain and coming to his feet started for their horses. The remaining pair, already upright, followed, sunlight glistening dully off their dark bodies. Vaulting onto their ponies they began to move off, one pausing to look back at the outlaws.

"Good," he said, apparently voicing thanks by the only white man's word he knew.

In the next instant the clearing rocked with the blast of a gunshot. The brave jolted on his pony, began to fall. A yell went up from his friends as Enright spun to face Jake Tolbert.

"What the hell did you do that for?" he asked in strangled tone. "They wasn't hurting nothing."

Tolbert was leveling his weapon at the back of the second fleeing Indian. "They make mighty fine running targets," he said and pressed off the shot. The buck threw up his arms and fell from his horse.

"Just like to keep my hand in," Tolbert said callously, drawing a bead on the last of the braves. "Kind of like hunting deer."

"For crissakes—ain't you done enough killing?" Enright shouted.

Tolbert lowered his forty-five, calmly began to reload the weapon. "Had to let that one go—out of range," he said. "But I reckon two out of three is good shooting."

Enright, shock visible on his lumpy features, was staring at Tolbert in disbelief. "Are you some kind of a looney?" he demanded. "Was no cause to shoot them poor Indians—same as there weren't no need for all that killing in Prescott and for shooting down them folks in Springerville! Now, I don't say a man oughtn't use his gun when it's needful, but to just up and—"

"We can end this partnership any time!" Tolbert snarled, suddenly angry as he shoved his pistol back into the holster. "You've got your share of the gold—I've got mine. Nothing to keep you from climbing aboard your horse and riding on."

Enright's mouth tightened. He shook his head. "Naw, we best stay together, I expect—leastwise till we get to Texas."

Tolbert was again his quiet, icy self. "Up to you, but from now on keep your bellyaching to yourself. I do as I damn please—when I please."

Bone Enright shrugged. "Sure, Jake, it's just that I don't hold with shooting down a man when it ain't necessary. Hell, them braves wasn't even armed."

The cigar Tolbert had placed between his teeth was still unlit. Striking a match the outlaw held the small flame to the tip of the

113

weed and brought it to life, his eyes on several scrub jays quarreling noisily in a pine nearby.

"When did you get to be such a Indian lover?" he asked, coming to his feet. "You got yourself a pretty little squaw stashed away somewhere?"

"Nope," Enright said, "just that I don't see—"

"Time we got to moving," Tolbert cut in, glancing at the sun. "You think we're in New Mexico, or are we still in Arizona?"

"New Mexico, I expect," Enright replied in a disgruntled voice and began to collect the eating and cooking utensils, dropping them into a sack. "Maybe not much, but some."

"Good," Tolbert murmured, blowing wavering blue smoke rings into the still air. "I'm glad to get out of Arizona."

"Same here," Bone agreed. *And I'll be damn glad to get away from you,* he added mentally.

Shooting down a man in a fight or for something you wanted bad was one thing— killing him just for the hell of it was something else. Tolbert, he'd finally come to realize, needed no reason whatever—and that was an uncomfortable thought.

12

It was typical of John Rye to put out of his mind thoughts of Pearly Joplin and all else other than those centering on the capturing and bringing to justice of Jake Tolbert and Bone Enright as he rode out of Springerville.

It had been Tolbert and Enright who had murdered the storekeeper and his wife, the lawman was certain. All the signs reflecting the needless brutality of the pair, particularly Tolbert, were there. Admittedly Bone Enright and their young partner, Gillespie, were killers, but only Tolbert, living up to the reputation he'd acquired in the past few years as a vicious murderer—according to the sheriff in Prescott—would have so needlessly slain the Springerville storekeeper and his wife.

Rye's features hardened as he thought of Tolbert. The outlaw was not entitled to live—even long enough to be hanged, much less tried. He should be shot down on sight, killed, so that there would be no chance of some tenderhearted judge being persuaded by a clever lawyer to spare his life or of some careless deputy allowing him to escape.

It would be difficult to not put a bullet in Jake Tolbert when he finally caught up with him, and Rye had a quick wish that he hadn't been handed the chore of bringing the outlaw in. It was unfair to place that responsibility on his shoulders—but then the governor of Arizona Territory was unaware of the past, of what had gone before.

Rye brushed at his jaw, tipped his hat forward over his eyes to minimize the glare, and scanned the trail ahead. He could not see too far, a mile or so, perhaps, because of the undulating, brushy terrain and the winding course the trail followed.

He could not expect the outlaws to be in sight, anyway as they had almost a full day's start on him. But as before, that fact mattered little to the lawman. He would bring the pair in no matter how long it took—not only because of the crimes they had committed, but because of his hatred for Jake Tolbert.

Tolbert . . . The marshal shook his head in an unconscious effort to dislodge the thought of the outlaw and what it did to him and so clear his mind. It had taken years to do just that—to relegate the man to the dark, remote recesses of his memory where he would be forgotten, but the effort had now failed. Tolbert was again a part of his life, an undeniable factor that he, as a lawman, had to contend with.

Vague rumors of the man and his activities had reached him during recent months, but Rye had resolutely kept them from his mind—but that could not be the way of it now. Eventually—soon—he would come face to face with Jake Tolbert, the old wound would be raked open, and the urge to kill the man—after first torturing him, making him beg for mercy—would lay its overpowering pressure on John Rye.

The recollection of the outlaw's handsome face floated before the lawman's eyes—not as he looked now but as he had during those days years back when they had both lived in the river-front city of St. Louis. Tolbert had been a gambler then, an expert in his profession, a man always with a pocketful of money and the object of many women's attention.

The war had come to an end and Rye, seeking to support his wife, Beth, had at first taken a job as a deputy sheriff in a settlement not far from St. Louis. As it paid but little and the rewards for outlaws were large, he soon became a bounty hunter.

The work took him away from home for lengthy periods of time during which Beth was left alone in their small cottage. Rye hadn't been aware that Jake Tolbert even knew of Beth—petite, dark hair, clear blue eyes, a striking figure, and a skin soft as rose petals—until he returned one day and found her gone. A note told him she could no longer stand the loneliness, that she was going away with a man she had met one day on the street—one who could give her all the things she was being deprived of.

At first John Rye flew into a fury and on making inquiries, learned that during his absence a man had been seen coming to the house every day, that he was a tall, well-dressed, handsome individual, said to be a successful gambler. Rye, checking further into the matter learned the interloper's name was Jake Tolbert. His anger had soared with that information. He knew of Tolbert, had seen him in the gaming houses, and while his reputation as an honest, square gambler was admitted, his fame as a woman chaser was equally well known.

Rye at first made plans to track down the couple, bring Beth to her senses even if it called for a shootout with Tolbert, but reason quickly prevailed and he abandoned the thought. He had neglected Beth, left her alone sometimes for months while he pursued his way of making a living. If this was what she wanted, then let it be so. A life with Tolbert evidently appealed to her—his unsavory reputation notwithstanding. And perhaps it would work out; Jake just might make her a good husband.

It hadn't turned out that way. Rye, returning to St. Louis a year or so later, was told by friends that word had come of Beth's death—a suicide the authorities in New Orleans, where she had been living, had reported. Beth had put a revolver to her temple and taken her own life.

Once more a killing anger had possessed John Rye. He had gone immediately to New Orleans determined to bring Tolbert to account, but the gambler had disappeared. Anyway, the U.S. marshal there had pointed out, Jake could not be charged with murder; he had not triggered the weapon that put an end to Beth's life. He no doubt was the cause, but he was not the perpetrator of the terrible thing.

Soon after that, Rye had assumed the position as a special U.S. marshal and embarked on the career that had made him famous as well as feared. He heard nothing of Jake Tolbert for a time; the man seemed to have dropped out of sight. And then later, an occasional rumor would crop up, one to the effect that Tolbert had forsaken gambling, his luck apparently having run out, and had become an outlaw.

It was a strange twist of fate, Rye thought, that he was on the trail of the man he hated so deeply; stranger yet that when he caught up with Tolbert he would be denied the vengeance he had once sought but put aside, the desire for which he now found coursing through him again. Instead he would have to protect and bring him in alive for the law to deal with. It would be a terrible moment for him when he threw down on Jake Tolbert; the urge to pull the trigger of the weapon he'd be holding would be near irresistible —that was the way it must be.

First, however, he had to catch up with

Tolbert and his outlaw partner before anything could come to pass, and to accomplish that, Rye continued well on into the evening, halting late to make a dry camp and rest the chestnut and then back in the saddle and on the trail again at first light.

He could still see no signs of the outlaws ahead although there were times when fairly open country offered long vistas of the road and surrounding area. But they were there, the lawman was confident—keeping out of sight and steadily on the move.

Late in the morning Rye topped out a fair rise and drew to a stop. Two horses stood motionless in the hot sunlight a short distance off the trail. Near one he thought he could see a sprawled body.

Circling quietly, careful to keep in the brush that surrounded the small clearing, the lawman made an approach. It was a body, he saw when he got near—an Indian. Glancing about he spotted the lifeless form of a second brave.

Rye dismounted a few yards from the first body, tethered the chestnut to a small fir, and, still within the concealing cover of brush, stood quiet and listened for several minutes. Convinced there was no one around, the marshal crossed to where the

Indian lay face down on the thin grass. He had been shot once in the back, Rye saw, and noted also that the brave had no weapon other than a skinning knife.

Leaving the body, dead for probably a day or so, Rye moved to the other Indian—now the object of attention of several vultures, unnoticed earlier, perched on a lightning-shattered pine a short distance away. Rye drove the big, broad-winged scavengers off with a wave of his hat and made his quick examination. Like the first brave, this one had been shot in the back and carried no weapon other than a knife.

The lawman stood quiet for a time thinking about the dead men, endeavoring to figure out what had taken place. Why would anyone shoot down two apparently harmless Indians?

A thought came to him suddenly. Pivoting, Rye returned to the first brave. There, moving slowly about in a widening circle, he located the remainder of what had been a camp. Besides the blackened ashes he found two spent brass cartridges, a cigar butt, and the bootheel prints of two men.

The lawman's features hardened. It looked like the work of the two outlaws he was following—most probably of Tolbert. Jake would need no reason to kill the Indians, would do so on the spur of the moment, if all the things said about him could be believed—and John Rye was certain they could be.

Grim, he dragged the corpses into a nearby wash, laid them side by side, and then caved in the walls of the narrow cut to cover the bodies. Dissatisfied with the results since the braves were not well covered, the lawman brought up some brush, threw it into the ravine, and weighted it down with several rocks that were handy.

That task finally completed, he turned to the Indians' horses, standing idly by. Neither was wearing a saddle, but both had make-shift bridles with trailing ropes that could become entangled in the brush and bring about death in one form or another. He'd remove the bridles and thus permit them to graze without the dangerous impediments.

But the Indian ponies, repelled by the scent of a white man, refused to let him approach, both shying away each time he drew near. Acutely aware of the need to be back on the trail in pursuit of Tolbert and Enright, who, he felt certain, had two more brutal murders to their credit, Rye gave up the idea of helping the wiry little ponies and returning to his horse shook the reins free, mounted, and rode on.

He'd lost an hour and a half or so, Rye guessed, and that wasn't good. But in taking time to bury the Indians, he'd done what a man should do.

13

"Hey—Bone!"

The shout coming from the shadowy brush growing on a slope adjacent to the trail brought Enright and Tolbert to a halt.

"Who the hell are they?" Tolbert demanded sourly as three riders appeared and came down the grade toward them.

Enright was grinning with pleasure. "Old *compadres* of mine from 'way back. One with a face like a horse is Ira Sanderson. Old codger with all the gray hair next to him is Gabe Potter. That hard-looking skinny one's called Tennessee. Ain't never heard no other name."

Tolbert spat, shook his head. "I don't

want them teaming up with us—makes too big a party," he warned. "And keep your trap shut about the gold we're carrying."

"Where you headed, old son?" Sanderson shouted as he and the two men with him drew to a stop directly in front of Enright. "Last time I seen you, you was hightailing it out of El Paso at a high lope with the law nipping at your ass."

"Didn't catch me for damn sure!" Enright grinned and jerked a thumb at his partner. "Boys, this here's Jake Tolbert, friend of mine. I've done told him who you are."

Tolbert nodded coldly. Sanderson nodded and moved forward, hand extended in greeting. Jake coolly ignored the gesture. As Sanderson pulled back, Gabe Potter shrugged.

"You're running with mighty highfalutin friends, Bone," he said. "What makes him figure he's too good to shake a man's hand?"

"He don't mean nothing by it," Enright replied hurriedly. "It's just that we been riding mighty hard and we're both a mite tuckered."

"Riding hard from who?" Sanderson wanted to know, rolling a cigarette.

Enright's mouth tightened. "That bastard

of a marshal—John Rye,'' he said.

"Rye?'' Potter echoed. "He in these parts?''

"Is, for a fact. Was a shooting back in a little town over Arizona way—Show Low. Me and Jake sort of upset things. Next thing we knew Rye was trailing us.''

"Had to be something real special to put him on your tails,'' the slim gunman called Tennessee observed dryly. "You sure there weren't nothing more to it than a shooting?''

"That's all,'' Tolbert stated flatly before Enright could answer.

"Gillespie—you all recollect him,'' Enright continued after the pause that followed Jake Tolbert's bloodless words. "He was with us. Got his. Rye killed him.''

"Damn!'' Potter exclaimed. "Knew Rye was fast with his iron but I would've figured Gillespie faster. Rye must've somehow got the drop on him.''

"Ain't sure about that one way or the other, but Gillespie's dead.''

"Tough,'' Tennessee said, producing his makings and starting a smoke. "Was a younker but plenty good to ride the river with. I recollect he always notched his bullets. Claimed that give them a heap more power.''

"Rye putting him under—that's hard to believe," Potter murmured, pulling off his hat and running fingers through his hair. "Mighty hard."

"Well, it's true," Enright stated firmly, twisting about in his saddle. "Done told you—we was running together—"

"Ain't misdoubting you—just can't savvy how or—"

—"Well," Sanderson said, "I reckon that just adds to the score I got against him—and that I'm hoping to settle someday."

"We've all got a score to settle with him," Tennessee said, blowing smoke into the late afternoon air. "He's been pussyfooting around this country long enough. I'm ready to call it quits—have it out with him."

A long minute of silence followed the younger man's words. Finally Enright shook his head.

"I ain't so sure you're talking smart, Tennessee. Rye's gone up against the best guns I can think of, and he always comes out on top. You're plenty fast, I know, but I ain't sure you can beat him."

"Maybe it's about time I was finding out," the gunman declared. "Like I said, I'm plumb tired of dodging him."

"I'm feeling the same way," Tolbert said,

coming into the discussion. "Rye's got to be a damn nuisance."

Sanderson and the others considered that remark for several moments. Tennessee broke the silence. "Reckon he's a bit more'n that. Every time I turn around lately, damned if he ain't somewheres close."

"This would be a good time to change that," Tolbert went on his quiet, even way. "Three of you—all good with your guns, I take it. You could climb back up there on the slope and surprise him like you did Bone and me."

"Yeh, I reckon we could," Tennessee drawled. "Now, what about you and Bone? Where'll you be? Seems you ought to ring yourselves in on the party, too."

"Sure be smart to get as many guns lined up against him as we can muster," Sanderson said.

"I'm still wondering why you and Bone don't throw in with us on it," Tennessee pressed, his attention still on Tolbert.

Jake's shoulders stirred indifferently. "Bone and me's got to get to Texas—Fort Worth—in a hurry. There's some important business we have to take care of."

"What kind of business?" Potter wanted to know, a suspicious note in his voice.

129

"Personal," Tolbert said and looked off over the hills.

"How about it, Bone?" Potter said, turning to Enright. "Sounds like a right good idea to me. You willing to throw in with us and put a cork in this here tin star's jug? Or is that there business in Fort Worth too important?"

Enright scratched at the stubble on his jaw. "Well, maybe it would be a right good idea," he said sidling a glance at Tolbert. "Ganging up on Rye ought to make it easy. What do you say, Jake? Can we take the time?"

Tolbert was still gazing out over the land, eyes apparently on a hawk soaring lazily in a wide circle above a grassy hollow where a rabbit or some other small animal had caught its sharp attention. He would have preferred to ride on—with or without Bone Enright—and let the gunman Tennessee and his friends take care of John Rye.

But not being a part of it after what that fool Enright said could create suspicion; and with twenty thousand dollars gold in his saddlebags, Tolbert wanted to avoid trouble with the likes of Bone's friends at all cost. Riding on alone wouldn't be smart either. Enright just might tell Sanderson and the

130

others about the gold. Besides, why should he pass up the chance to get Rye out of his life once and for all time?

"I don't see that another day or so getting to Fort Worth will make any difference," he said, now warming up strongly to the idea. "Only thing, I'm not dead sure Rye's trailing us. Covered up our tracks real good."

"Well, there's somebody coming," Sanderson said, pointing back up the trail.

All turned their eyes to the west. A lone rider, much too distant for identification, had just topped out a rise and moved into view.

"That him, you reckon?" Tennessee asked.

"If he's been dogging Bone and Jake, you can bet on it," Sanderson said in a positive, resigned way.

Enright swore. "Knew damn well we oughtn't to've hauled up and made camp last night," he said, wagging his head. "Should've kept right on riding."

"Maybe it ain't Rye," Tennessee said. "Lot of pilgrims use this road."

"I expect it's him, all right," Tolbert said quietly. Now that he realized the advantages to him personally in the plan, he wasn't about to let Enright and the others lose courage and back out. "We won't get another chance like this—not in a lifetime."

"Tolbert's right," Sanderson said.

"Then we best be getting off the road, out of sight—"

"For certain," Potter agreed. "I recollect a place on down the road a piece where it gets real narrow. Slopes come in on both sides. Be a good place to set up an ambush."

"Sounds just right," Sanderson said. "How we doing it? We all just opening up on him when he gets where we want him?" the outlaw added as, in a group, they moved on.

"Best way for sure," Tolbert said.

Potter shook his head. "Nope—that'll be going too easy on him. I say we make him pay for all the trouble he's caused us—and for killing Gillespie and a couple more of the boys."

"How?" Sanderson wanted to know.

"By stringing him up, that's how! Giving him a dose of this here law he's so damned set on."

Tennessee bobbed. "Now, that sounds mighty interesting! We could hold us a trial, have a judge, and a jury, and everything—"

"I ain't so sure about that," Enright cut in doubtfully. "I'm thinking it'd be better to just up and blow him out of the saddle. He's tricky. Fooling around with him like that—he maybe'll get away, slick as he is.''

"How the hell could he? There'll be five of us a-crowding him. We'll pull his fangs first off, then put a rope on him. Sure won't be able to do nothing then," Potter pointed out.

"Ain't no danger of him getting away, once we hogtie him," Sanderson said. And then added enthusiastically, "Let's do this here thing up right! Let's take him on to Jessup's Place and hold the trial and hanging there."

"Jessup's Place—where's that?" Enright asked as they approached the cut in the mountainside through which the trail passed.

"Kind of a town on down the road a piece," Potter explained. "Ain't a real town, I reckon—just a saloon and a store run by this friend of ours, Leo Jessup. We was there this morning."

"Seems to me we're going to a lot of extra trouble," Tolbert said, having the same thoughts as Enright.

Sanderson turned to him. "Going to be worth it. That bastard's got it coming, considering all the trouble he's caused us. Anyway, why not us have a little fun doing

133

it—sort of like a celebration?"

"You're dang right there, Ira!" Potter said. "Us getting rid of him calls for a celebration—a real jimdandy!"

"And Jessup's just the place to hold it. Plenty of liquor and women—"

"Which costs money," Tolbert interrupted. "And Bone and me are a little short on cash."

"Don't fret none about that," Sanderson said with a wave of his hand. "If you're busted, me and Potter and Tennessee will stake you to a couple of bottles. And the Jessup girls come cheap, if you're of a mind to spend some time with one."

"Can even run your credit up some with Jessup," Potter said. "Just tell him you'll be back through in a couple of days with plenty of cash to spend."

"We'll be obliged to you for staking us," Tolbert said, with a glance at Enright. "Do the same for you some day."

"Well, we won't be keeping books on it," Sanderson said. "A friend's a friend, I always say . . . Now, we best be getting all set. Rye'll be showing up here before we know it."

14

There was a rider on the trail behind him, Rye saw a time later, as the chestnut reached the crest of a long upgrade. There was no way of telling who it was, for at that moment the horse and rider at such a distance were merely small, dark blurs silhouetted against the afternoon skyline.

No doubt it was just some pilgrim or possibly a cowhand on his way to the next town. That it could be either Tolbert or Enright having pulled off to one side of the road and waited as a means for getting behind him was not likely, the lawman believed. He had located the hoofprints of two horses leaving the clearing where the

Indians had been killed, and having watched the trail closely for any indication of the outlaws leaving it—and seeing none so far—Rye was certain the pair was still in front of him; and that was all that mattered.

It was fortunate for the pilgrim that he was in back and not ahead of him, the lawman thought, his glance continually sweeping the country unfurled around him for an ambush. Tolbert was a trigger-happy madman who had proven he'd as soon shoot down a man as look at him. Getting to the outlaw before he could kill again was important. Of course, Bone Enright could be equally as vicious, but all indications led the lawman to believe he was not.

Rye rode on, constantly on the alert. A sort of wariness had come over him from the time he'd entered an area of broken hills where the brush crowded up close to the trail on both sides, and there were numerous narrow cuts in the mountain through which it passed. But never once did he see anything that disturbed him or put him on guard. Jays and other birds flitted in and out of the trees, squirrels dashed across the trail in front of the chestnut, and all seemed normal in the bright, afternoon sunlight.

Abruptly, as he was passing through a

narrow cleft where the slopes of two brushy hills met to form an arroyo-like junction, a burst of gunshots off to the right brought the marshal to a halt. Hand resting on the butt of his pistol he wheeled, headed slowly toward the source of the reports.

In the next moment he reeled in the saddle from a blow to the head. Struggling to maintain his senses, Rye twisted about to fight off two men who had seized him and were dragging him off his horse. Two more closed in from either side. One was Enright, Rye saw as he began to fall. Tolbert appeared then, coming in from the right. It had been him apparently who fired the shots.

The lawman struck the ground with stunning force. A booted foot drove into his middle exploding breath from his lungs. Another sharp blow to the head from a gun butt sent his senses reeling once more. Someone yanked him roughly about, pulled his hands together behind his back, and bound them securely. A third rap to the head sent consciousness waning again. As if from a distance he heard a voice.

"Damn it, Gabe—don't kill him. Save him for the lynching party."

Gabe . . . Gabe Potter. Rye struggled to organize his scattered wits. He thought he'd recognized the man—a small-time, two-bit horse thief—when he was being dragged off the chestnut. And there was another one besides Tolbert and Bone Enright that had looked familiar—a gunman named Tennessee.

"Get the sonofabitch on his feet!" someone ordered.

Rye felt himself being jerked upright. A rope was looped about his body and pulled tight, pinning his arms to his sides. Head clearing fast, he glanced around at the men gathered about him.

Tolbert, no longer the handsome man he was in St. Louis, clothing old and worn, stood with folded arms, a smirk pulling at the corners of his mouth. Beside him was Enright, and at Enright's shoulder was another familiar face that was on the law's list of wanted outlaws—Ira Sanderson. But it was on Tolbert that Rye centered his mounting anger and hatred.

"This meeting's been a long time coming," he said in a low voice. "Luck's with you—you've got plenty of help."

Tolbert shrugged. "It's the other way around. Their being here keeps me from putting a bullet in you right now."

Sanderson bobbed. "That's for true,

138

Marshal. We're holding you for a trial."

"Trial?"

"Yeh. You're so almighty set on hauling everybody up before some judge and getting us sentenced to hang, we figured we'd just put the boot on the other foot and give you a dose of your own medicine."

"And that ain't all," Gabe Potter added. "You put under some mighty good friends of ours—Ed Gillespie for one, so Bone and his friend Jake there tells us. We aim to try you for killing them, just the way the law would."

Rye shrugged. "Kill me and there'll be another marshal to take my place."

"Maybe," Tennessee said indifferently. "But it'll be a spell before anybody 'cepting us and the bunch at Jessup's knows about it—and them and us sure ain't never going to do any blabbing."

All the while the conversation was taking place John Rye's eyes, glowing with a bitter hatred, were on Jake Tolbert. It was inevitable, he supposed, that in trailing the two outlaws, he'd ride into a trap set by the pair, and he had been prepared, more or less, to meet an emergency, but he had not anticipated the help they had managed to recruit. He wondered if their getting together had been a spur-of-the-moment arrangement or had been planned ahead of time.

Regardless, the last verse of the song hadn't been sung yet. Rye didn't know how but in some way he would free himself and finish the job of bringing in Jake Tolbert. Doing the same with Bone Enright was a secondary obligation, and there was no hard-and-fast order to bring him in alive as there was with Tolbert. He'd do so if at all possible; however, if it meant putting a bullet in Enright to get Jake Tolbert back to Prescott still breathing, he'd not hesitate.

First things came first, though; he must find a way to escape from the party of outlaws. Maybe it would come later, at a place they were calling Jessup's, where they intended to hold a mock trial, try him for shooting some of their owlhoot friends —Gillespie for one. Perhaps his chance would come then.

"Come on, come on—ain't no sense standing here jawing," Ira Sanderson said impatiently. "Let's get back to Jessup's and start things to cooking."

Potter and Tennessee, seizing Rye's arms, assisted him onto his horse while Sanderson and Enright brought up their mounts. All climbed into their saddles, and then, with

Rye flanked by Sanderson and Enright, preceded by Tennessee, and followed by Tolbert and Potter, they struck out along the road in an easterly direction.

"Sure did enjoy that woman of yours," Rye heard Tolbert say in a sly voice. "Got to say she was about the prettiest I ever came across."

The lawman stiffened despite an effort to make it appear he had not heard.

"His woman?" Enright said, turning half about in his saddle. "You saying you was fooling around with Rye's wife?"

"Took her away from him," Tolbert replied. "Was real easy."

"Well, I'll be damned! Where is she now?"

"Dead. I got tired of her after a while. Tried to kick her out of my place, make her go on back home. Wouldn't do it, no matter how much slapping around I handed her. Finally settled it one day. Left a loaded pistol where she could find it real easy. Blew her own brains out with it one night when I was off with another woman."

It was all being said for his benefit to taunt him, Rye knew, but such knowledge did not lessen the impact nor diminish the anger that rocked through him. He had suspected most of what Tolbert had said, now had it confirmed; the chore of keeping Jake Tolbert alive to face the hangman was suddenly a hundred times more difficult than it had been at the start.

"Thought you'd like to know what happened to your little Beth," Tolbert continued. "Expect you've done a lot of wondering about her."

Rye could no longer control his hate. "I hope you burn an extra day in hell for what you put her through," he ground out savagely. "I'll see you hang—and enjoy every moment of it."

They were turning off the road, the lawman saw settling back into his saddle, heading up a short slope to a flat on which a fairly large, barnlike house surrounded by brush and trees and with several small huts at its rear could be seen. As the party swung into the hitchrack at the side of the main structure, an elderly man with a chest-length beard, white hair shining in the sunlight, and sweat glistening off his shirtless torso came out onto the porch to greet them. A half-dozen scantily clad women quickly gathered about him.

"Hey you all!" he shouted, jamming hands into the pockets of his stained denim pants. "Sure didn't look for you back so soon!"

Rye, sullen anger simmering within him, sat quietly in his saddle while the chestnut and the other horses were tethered to the rack's crossbar.

"Wasn't aiming to be back," Sanderson replied, "but we got us something real important to do." Seizing Rye by the arm he dragged him off his horse, righted the off-balance lawman, and then, standing beside him, placed a hand on his shoulder. "This here's John Rye—the big muckity-muck lawman some folks call the Doomsday Marshal."

"Is that a fact," Jessup said sardonically.

"We're aiming to hold us a court here in your place, try him for killing some friends of ours—then string him up—just like they do in a regular court."

"Sounds right interesting, don't it, girls?" Jessup said, glancing about at the women. "We'll be right happy to accommodate you. I ain't never been one to have any use for no badge-toter, no matter what kind. Now, you just tell me what you want done, and we'll hop to it."

"Be needing a jury, for one thing," Gabe

Potter said. "Supposed to have twelve men."

"Well, we ain't got no twelve men around—there's maybe five or six inside. Just have to use some of my girls. Good as any man, anyway."

"Better," one of the women said, and all laughed.

Sanderson, the other outlaws having finished with securing their mounts, gave Rye a shove, sent him stumbling toward the two steps that led up to the porch fronting Jessup's.

"Get inside," the outlaw said harshly. "We're going to show you what it's like standing up before a judge and hearing yourself told you're going to swing."

"Misdoubt he'll care much once that rope snaps his neck," Tennessee observed dryly as they all climbed up onto the landing and moved for the open doorway.

15

Jessup's Place was large. It consisted of a bar that angled across a back corner, had ankle-deep sawdust on the floor fronting the counter. Calendars graced the walls along with numerous deer antlers, and at least two dozen tables with accompanying chairs were scattered about the room.

There was no area reserved for dancing, a diversion, according to the bearded proprietor, that was sinful and a tool of the devil. The fact that he maintained a stable of nearly nude women for the enjoyment of his patrons—cowhands, lumberjacks, drifters, and outlaws—was entirely acceptable to his way of thinking.

"Get them lamps lit!" Jessup shouted to a swamper slouched in a chair at the end of the bar. "Too dang dark in here to hold a court!"

Aching and still a bit groggy from the blows he had taken, Rye was pushed and shoved into the rank-smelling, smoky room. Steadying himself, he glanced about. Among the half-dozen men in the place were several familiar faces, all small-time outlaws just as were Sanderson and the two men who were with him. The bartender looked familiar also, but the lawman could not peg him and spent no time trying to.

"Ain't that the tin star they call the Doomsday Marshal?" called one of the patrons, a tall, smooth-shaven man, as Potter pushed Rye onto one of the chairs.

"It sure is," Bone Enright responded. "The genuine article. He sure don't look so fierce right now, does he?"

"What're you going to do with him?"

"We're putting him on trial, that's what," Ira Sanderson said. "He's going to get a taste of this here law he's so damned proud of."

The man who had asked the question rose to his feet. "Hell, he's a U.S. marshal. I ain't sure I want to have anything to do with this."

"Then get the hell out of here," Gabe Potter snapped. "We don't want nobody on this here jury that ain't got the guts to do what's needful."

The tall man nodded and, tight lipped, crossed the saloon to its entrance and disappeared into the closing day. The swamper had lowered the big wagonwheel chandeliers and was lighting the lamps. Sanderson and Potter, satisfied with the arrangement of chairs for their jury, were now putting a table in front of Rye and placing a seat behind it for a judge—whoever he was to be. Jessup came up at that moment, a bung starter in his hand, which he laid on the table.

"This here's the judge's gavel," he said and, laughing, banged the table sharply with it.

Several of the women moved in for a better look at Rye, silent and unyielding in his chair, hands still bound behind him, rope now loose about his waist and in a pile on the floor behind him.

Tolbert, alone at one of the tables, had a bottle and glass for company, the lawman noted. The outlaw's shuttered eyes were on his partner, Bone Enright, seated a few steps away with one of the girls on his lap. Farther over, Rye could see the gunman Tennessee, also with a woman, while Sanderson and Potter busily continued to create their idea of a courtroom. The men who were present in Jessup's at the beginning were taking no hand in the proceedings but remained slumped in their chairs and silently looked on.

The circle of lamps lit, the swamper crossed to the far side of the room and, grasping the rope attached by way of a pulley to the wheel, pulled the arrangement back to its high level. As the man tied off the rope, Jessup clapped his hands loudly.

"Reckon we're all ready!" he shouted.

Sanderson nodded. "Let's get it going, then. Jessup, how about you being the judge?"

The bearded saloon owner bowed low. "I'd be mighty honored to be him," he said and moved to the table and chair set aside for his use.

"Need twelve of you people for the jury," Sanderson went on, gesturing at the half circle of empty seats in the center of the room. "Some of you get up here now and do your bounden duty."

Three of the patrons arose, swaggered over to the designated chairs, and sat down. They

148

were followed at once by a like number of the women.

"Got to have six more," Sanderson announced.

"Bone, how about you and your partner. Ain't you getting in on this?"

Enright, pushing the girl off his lap to her feet, and clinging to her hand as if fearing she might vanish, started to take a place on the panel. Midway he paused and looked back at Tolbert.

"You coming, Jake?"

Tolbert shook his head and sullenly regarded his glass of whiskey. Enright shrugged and, with his girl friend, continued on to the half circle and took their places.

"Ain't got enough jurors here," Sanderson said, glancing about. "Sure want to give the marshal here a fair trial. Now we—"

"Count me and Tennessee in," Gabe Potter said as he and the gunman settled onto vacant chairs. "Hell, I reckon you've got more'n enough now to hang him."

"That's for damn sure!" Tennessee said. "Let's get this thing to going—I got other business on my mind!"

Sanderson waved his hands for silence as the room filled with shouts and laughter.

"All right, I reckon we can get at it. You ready, Judge?"

"Ready!" Jessup replied and banged the table before him with the bung starter. "Who's talking first?"

"Me," Sanderson answered, taking a pull at the bottle he was holding by the neck. "I'm the one that'll be telling all you jury people, and you, too, Judge, about this here killer." The outlaw paused, set the bottle on a nearby bench, and moved to a position in front of Rye. Pointing a finger at the lawman, he continued. "You saying you never shot down a fine young fellow named Gillespie?"

Rye made no reply. In no way would he dignify the ludicrous proceedings with an answer, nor would he lower himself by protesting anything that was said or done.

"You ain't saying nothing, are you?" Sanderson declared loudly. "That plain means you're guilty—guilty as sin of murdering that young fellow. And there's some others I can name—all good men."

Despite the gravity of his position, a half smile tugged at Rye's lips. *Good men!* All would have been killers, just like Gillespie —outlaws of the worst kind—otherwise he would not have been sent to bring them in.

"Ain't you going to say something, prisoner?" Jessup demanded, again hammering on the table with his makeshift gavel.

Rye maintained his stony silence. Jessup nodded and made a sweeping gesture at Sanderson.

"You got some witnesses to this here killing? We sure got to be fair to the prisoner."

"Yes, sir," Sanderson replied with elaborate politeness. "I'm betting there ain't one man under this roof that don't know firsthand about the accused doing some killing. But take Bone Enright there on the jury, he seen him kill this young fellow Gillespie only a couple of days ago. Stand up, Bone, and speak your piece."

Enright got to his feet. "Was over Arizona way. Town folks call Show Low. Me and Jake Tolbert—he's the man setting over there by hisself—and Gillespie was in a saloon having ourselves a drink and talking about old times when this here mar—prisoner come waltzing in. Didn't say nothing. Just dragged out his iron and started shooting. Killed Gillespie deader than a doornail."

"Gillespie shoot at him?" Sanderson

151

asked, reaching for his bottle.

"Nope, never got no chance—"

"All right, set down," Jessup directed and shifted his attention to Tolbert. "You was there. You got anything to say?"

Jake Tolbert made no effort to respond, simply sat in morose silence. Jessup glanced at Rye.

"What've you got to say about it? You kill this here Gillespie like they say?"

"What the hell difference does it make what he says—he's guilty. Go ahead, string him up!" one of the men sitting at a table yelled. "Far as I'm concerned, you can string up every tin star in the country!"

Jessup fixed his watery eyes on Rye. "You guilty or ain't you?"

"Hold on there, Judge," Sanderson said before the lawman, had he been so inclined, could reply. "That's for the jury to decide. Up to you to tell us to hang him."

Jessup bobbed vigorously. "You're right," he said and motioned to the jurors. "You got a verdict?"

"Sure do," Bone Enright said, assuming the role of foreman. "He's guilty—just as guilty as he can be."

Jessup fixed the others seated in the half

circle with his baleful stare. "That right? You all say he's guilty as sin?"

There was a chorus of agreement accompanied by much laughter and talk. Jessup banged on his table and put his attention on Rye.

"Then there ain't nothing left for this here court to do but sentence this here desperate outlaw to swing—to hang by his neck till he's dead."

Gabe Potter leaped to his feet. "Let's get at it!"

"No," Sanderson said, again waving his hands for quiet as others took up a noisy approval of Potter's words. "Ain't decent to just up and lynch a man right off. He needs to set around, think of all the bad things he's gone and done, and be sorry for it."

"That's right," Jessup declared. "I sentence this here outlaw to wait till morning."

"Where'll we keep him?" someone asked. "We ain't got no jail—unless we use one of the girls' shacks—"

"I'm expecting them to be real busy with all you jaspers around," Jessup said with a broad grin, "so I can't spare no shack for that. That big tree out front'll have to be the jail. Can tie him to it, then come sunup can

hang him from it. Be real convenient . . .
Now, belly up to the bar. First round's on
me. After that I'm expecting you to pay.''

16

Shouts of approval greeted Jessup's invitation, and, as one, all of the men and women in the saloon, with the exception of Jake Tolbert, gravitated to the bar. Jessup himself, after a moment, stepped in behind the counter to assist the man who regularly handled the chore of pouring drinks.

Rye watched it all through half-closed eyes. A grimness still masked his chiseled features, and the cold, hard hatred he had for the outlaws—all outlaws—continued to pulse steadily through him. The so-called trial was not in his thoughts—it was but an incident not worth remembering, nor was the verdict anything of consequence.

They had intended to kill him from the start, and it surprised him somewhat that they had not just shot him down back there on the road. But one of them, he forgot which, had come up with the idea of holding a trial. That had been a break for him—and he must make the most of it. Rye was a man who believed that as long as he still breathed he had a chance to beat death—and right now he was far from giving up, despite the odds.

"What about the tin star?" someone shouted from the crowd gathered in front of the bar. "Ain't we supposed to treat him to a last drink?"

"Sure—why not?" another voice chimed in.

"Don't none of you go untying his hands!" Enright shouted hurriedly, stepping out of the group. "You want to give him a drink go ahead, but leave that cord around his wrists. He's a mighty tricky *hombre!*"

One of the saloon women, a shot glass of whiskey in one hand, separated herself from the bar and strutted up to the lawman.

"You wanting a drink, mister?" she asked in a bantering voice.

Rye made no answer, only stared at her through his narrowed eyes.

"Well, here's one for you," the woman said and threw the liquor into his stolid face.

A burst of laughter went up from others in the saloon. "Good for you, Nellie!" someone shouted.

The woman, blond, on the plump side, with broad hips and large, mostly uncovered breasts, pivoted and started back toward the bar.

"I ain't got no use for no lawman," she said, "and I sure ain't got no use for him, 'specially."

Rye, eyes smarting from the liquor, drops falling from his mustache and stubble of beard, did not change expression. He'd not give them the satisfaction of showing any pain or discomfort.

"You're all right, Nellie!" one of the men who had seated himself at a table, called. "He do something bad to you—maybe put a bullet in your man?"

Nellie, reaching the counter, leaned back against it. Turning to face Rye she shook her head. "Nope, he ain't never done nothing to me personally. It's just that I've heard a plenty about him, about this here 'doomsday' thing and how everybody's real scared of him. I was wanting to show him that here's somebody that ain't scared."

"That's the stuff, Nellie!" a voice called as more shouts went up following the woman's words. "Anytime you want to throw in with me and the boys, you just say so."

"Wouldn't be because I can ride and shoot a gun that you'd want me along," the woman snapped and rapped on the bar with her empty glass for a drink.

As more laughter filled the saloon Jessup came out from behind the counter, a drink in his hand, and approached Rye.

"I ain't got no use for a badge toter either," he said, "but I reckon a man in your boots is entitled to a swallow of good whiskey—knowing what's coming."

Rye shook his head.

"It gets mighty cold outside," Jessup continued, holding the glass to the lawman's mouth. "Best you take it."

Again the marshal declined. The saloon had quieted as everyone looked on. Jessup turned his head aside and spat at a nearby cuspidor in disgust.

"Have it your way, mister! I reckon you figure you're too good to have a drink on me. Well, come morning there'll be a big difference for sure—I'll be alive and you'll be dead, and all your highfalutin airs won't amount to powder smoke.''

Rye, maintaining his unwavering stolid expression, watched Jessup stalk off toward the bar. Tolbert, he noticed was still sitting alone at a table while Enright, with the same woman he had earlier made up to, had drawn well off to one side with her where he was engaging in an animated conversation.

Sanderson and Gabe Potter were slouched over the bar while between them the gunman Tennessee was posed with his elbows hooked on the edge of the counter as he stared emptily through the doorway. Abruptly he put his attention on Rye.

''Let's get that bastard the hell out of here!'' he yelled. ''I'm sick and tired of him looking at me.''

Immediately the crowd took up the gunman's suggestion. All came about and, following Tennessee's lead, crossed to where Rye sat affixed to his chair. For the first time since entering the saloon Jake Tolbert stirred himself, and while taking no active part in the proceedings, he joined the noisy, drunken crowd as they roughly pushed and dragged the lawman out into the darkening day and to the tree that was to be his jail.

''I recollect they got a jail tree like this over in a town in Arizona,'' a voice said.

"That'd be in Wickenburg," someone else volunteered. "They chain a man to a big mesquite—right down in the middle of the town 'cause they ain't got a regular jail."

Sanderson and Tennessee, each gripping an arm of John Rye, slammed him up against the pine and pushed him to a sitting position. As the slim gunman began to tie the rope to the the of the tree, Sanderson produced a length of rawhide cord. Pulling the marshal's feet together, he hobbled him effectively. Both outlaws, finishing their respective tasks, stepped back. Sanderson dusted his hands and grinned at Rye.

"I reckon that'll hold you till the sun's up," he said. "Meantime, you have yourself a real nice night."

Several laughs followed that. One of the women said, "We sure don't want you tired for the hanging."

The party hesitated as if expecting Rye to make a reply or perhaps voice a protest, but he remained quiet, returning glance for glance, and after a few moments all turned and headed back for the saloon. Tolbert alone did not immediately leave, nor did Bone Enright who, with his woman friend, halted on the porch of Jessup's and watched with interest as Jake sauntered over to where the marshal sat tethered, hobbled, with bound wrists, at the base of the pine tree.

"Was a pleasure knowing your wife," Tolbert said in a mocking voice and, leisurely pivoting on a heel, made his way back to the landing, mounted the steps, joined Enright and his woman who appeared to be awaiting him, and reentered the saloon.

Alone, John Rye fixed his attention on the west. The sun was down but full darkness would not come for another hour or so, and darkness, his one last hope of beating the outlaws at their game, of escaping and completing the job he was assigned to do, was a necessity. Stirring a bit to gain more comfort, he leaned back against the tree.

It had never really come to him—actually, he'd never thought about it—just how many enemies he had. Outlaws and their women and friends hated him with a passion, but how they felt was of no interest to Rye. They were scum, and the sooner the country was rid of them, one and all, the sooner civilization with its law and order would prevail and prosper. To help bring this about was his job.

A costly one, he thought somewhat bitterly, recalling Jake Tolbert's snide words of a few minutes earlier. He had lost Beth, the only woman he had ever cared about, and had done so unwittingly. Had he been aware of her loneliness, of her need for him, he would have forsaken the bounty-hunter trail and gotten himself hired on somewhere as a deputy sheriff or town marshal—a position that would have permitted him to be home most of the time.

But Beth had never mentioned it to him, and while he had known the hard, aching pain of loneliness too, he had stuck to his calling for the sake of the money it brought in. That was his error; in so doing he had opened the door for Jake Tolbert to move in on him, and Beth had succumbed to the gambler's charms.

Why hadn't he been smart enough to realize what his prolonged absences would bring about? He should have guessed Beth's life was a dreary one and taken the necessary steps to change it. They should have talked about it during the times he was home, but somehow it never occurred to him and Beth never complained. That had been the chief enemy and eventual downfall of their marriage, he reckoned—the lack of communication between them.

Rye shifted restlessly, glanced at the doorway of the saloon where lamplight was laying a rectangle on the floor of the porch. The racket within the place had increased, and behind it, two of the huts where the women lived and entertained showed light in their windows.

It was dark enough to make his move, the lawman decided—one that had to succeed or he was a dead man. Getting to his knees Rye worked himself around to the opposite side of the big pine where he would be less visible if someone in Jessup's took it upon themselves to come to the door and look his way.

Coming to his feet then, the lawman worked the rope confining him to the tree to one side. Taking another glance at Jessup's and seeing that all was clear, he doubled over and began to shake the upper part of his body vigorously.

Almost immediately the knife he carried beneath his armpit dislodged from its sheath and fell to the ground. With another look at the saloon's entrance to assure himself that he was not being seen, Rye quickly resumed a sitting posture much as before but now a bit more to the left so that his fingers could wrap themselves about the handle of the knife and retrieve it.

Maneuvering the blade about to where he

could slice through the cords that bound his wrists would not only take a bit of doing but require time as well. He had all night, or most of it—thanks to Ira Sanderson's insistence that the sentence of hanging be carried out just as it would have been by a regular court of law, at sunrise. If he used care and didn't let himself get caught by one of the outlaws while he worked at his bonds, he should be free well before daylight.

A shadow darkened the light in Jessup's doorway. Rye, the knife not yet in firm possession of his fingers, relaxed as one of the outlaws, Gabe Potter he thought, in company with a woman came out onto the landing. Watching narrowly, the lawman saw them come to the edge of the porch, pause. Both were very drunk, so much so that Potter had to steady himself by grasping one of the roof supports.

"He's there all right," the outlaw said thickly. "He ain't run off—"

"Ain't likely to," the woman responded in equally dragging tones. "Come on—let's go to my room."

The couple came off the porch and unsteadily made their way alongside the saloon toward the collection of huts at its rear. Rye kept his eyes on them until darkness swallowed them and then resumed the task of working the knife about to where the sharp edge of the blade was against the rawhide encircling his wrists and the handle was firm between his fingers. That accomplished the lawman began a patient sawing at the tough cords.

"Marshal—"

17

Bone Enright had spotted Gillespie's saddlebags on Rye's horse, too, Tolbert realized as he stared moodily at his partner. Enright was seated at a table a short distance away, his own saddlebags hung across the back of his chair, the saloon girl again on his lap. They were laughing and talking and having a big time, but Tolbert wasn't fooled; Enright was thinking about the gold the same as he was.

And fifteen thousand dollars' worth was a hell of lot better than seventy-five hundred which was what his share would be if he split it with Bone. Too, fifteen thousand added to the twenty thousand in his pouches would make a mighty fine stake.

Jake Tolbert's thoughts rambled on as the noise and confusion in the saloon mounted. The room was now heavy with smoke and the smell of spilled liquor, sweat, and coal oil, and somewhere in the hazy room a Jew's harp was being played, the high-pitched twanging barely audible in the racket.

Thirty-five thousand dollars in new gold coins—now that would give a man a real start in life again! He could return to St. Louis, to the Mississippi, in style and set himself up in a grand way. He could begin to live again the kind of gentleman's life he was accustomed to—and deserved.

And there'd be no loose ends hanging about to distract him. John Rye would be dead, and the lawman's ever-threatening shadow lodged in the back of his mind would be gone forever.

"You sure don't look like you're having yourself much of a time, mister!"

Tolbert raised his gaze, allowed his cold eyes to settle on Jessup. Well into his cups, the saloon man was being supported by one of his women—a tall, solidly built redhead.

"Why don't you pick yourself one of these here females of mine and start doing some living? Here—take Jenny," Jessup said and shoved the woman at Tolbert.

Stumbling, the woman came down hard on Tolbert's lap. The outlaw caught at the table to keep his chair from overturning with one hand, brushed Jenny off his legs and to the floor with the other, which, cursing and yelling, she hit with a thud.

"Damn you!" Jessup shouted, lurching toward Tolbert. "I don't let nobody slap my girls around!"

Tolbert's pistol was out and leveled before the bearded saloonkeeper could reach him. A hard smile cracked his lips.

"Back up, old man," he warned softly.

Jessup halted uncertainly, a frown on his florid features. After a moment he wagged his head. "Hell, I was only wanting you to have yourself a good time—"

The noise inside the saloon had tapered off at the first sign of trouble and now most everyone in the big room had gathered around the two men—all taking care, however, to not stand directly behind either Tolbert or Jessup.

"What say we just forget it?" Jessup suggested, a fixed smile on his face. "I ain't never been a man for hard feelings," he added and extended his hand.

Tolbert merely shrugged and looked away.

Jenny, sitting flat on the floor during the brief exchange of words, angrily got to her feet and whirled to Tolbert.

"You sonofabitch—who do you think you—" she began and then staggered back as Tolbert slapped her across the mouth, effectively silencing her tongue.

Several yells of protest went up from the crowd, but it got no further than that. Tolbert's cold, menacing appearance and the all-too-ready weapon still in his hand discouraged anything more than feeble verbal opposition.

The sneer was still on Tolbert's lips as the crowd began to drift away and the activity in the saloon resumed. He glanced covertly at Enright. The latter's absence from his side had been noticeable and Tolbert had a strong suspicion that his partner had hoped the confrontation with Jessup would end in gunplay with the saloon man coming out winner. After all, these were Enright's friends and ordinarily under the circumstances you'd think Enright would have taken his side.

But Enright hadn't—not that it mattered to Tolbert. He had no friends, and he wanted no friends—and he needed no help from any man alive. He'd always looked out for himself, and he expected he always would. Bone Enright apparently felt the same way.

Shouts rose abruptly above the din filling the saloon. Tolbert looked toward the source of the disturbance. It was Enright and the man, evidently a cowhand, at the table next him. They were on their feet locked in each other's arms, swaying back and forth as both endeavored to get a hand free as to strike a blow.

The two broke apart suddenly. Bone's opponent, quick to seize the advantage, drove a right to his jaw, rocking the outlaw back on his heels. Enright recovered immediately. With arms swinging he closed in on the cowhand. The pair came together and began to slug it out, toe to toe.

Tolbert glanced about. He was the only one in the saloon who had not hastened to form a ring around the two fighters and add his voice to the clamor being accorded the brawl. The realization that a hoped-for opportunity was at hand swept through him. Rising, he took up his saddlebags and sauntered toward the door. Reaching the entrance Jake hesitated, looked back, and, seeing that he was still unnoticed, he stepped out onto the landing.

There Jake Tolbert abandoned all pretense

of leisure. Hurriedly crossing the porch, he dropped off to ground level and walked quickly to the hitchrack. Shouldering the horse next to Rye's chestnut aside to gain room, the outlaw paused at the gelding's saddle and, working fast, unbuckled the near pocket of the saddlebags belonging to his one-time partner Gillespie, which Rye had taken possession of after the shooting at Show Low.

A curse slipped from his lips as he rummaged about in the leather pouch. Gillespie's bag of gold was not there. Circling the horse, Tolbert opened the pouch on the opposite side. Digging into it, pushing aside one or two items of clothing, he felt around. Shortly the tautness in his features faded when he located the bag of coins, and took it firmly in his grasp.

He hadn't been too sure that Rye would have Gillespie's share of the robbery. The lawman could have left it back in Springerville for safe keeping; luckily, for some reason he had not. But the fact that Rye did have Gillespie's saddlebags made it seem likely.

Unbuckling one of the pouches of his own saddlebags, Tolbert began to push aside some of the articles it contained and made

171

room for the bag containing Gillespie's share of the gold. One of the money belts Enright had got for them back at that general store where he'd shot the fool owner and his wife, which was now around his waist, was packed full. It had failed by far to hold all of the double eagles, and he had resorted to distributing a few in the various pockets of his clothing, leaving the remainder in the bank sack still in his saddlebag. Enright had followed a like procedure.

Coming about, Tolbert headed for Jessup's porch, having brief thoughts of mounting up and riding on alone while he had the chance, but discarding the idea as not only unwise but dangerous. On impulse—in the event Enright or someone else should note his absence and look for him—Tolbert changed directions and crossed to the tree where Rye was tied.

The lawman was slumped against the pine, his hating eyes cut down to narrow slits, his hard-cornered features barely visible in the pale light. Tolbert, now fifteen thousand dollars richer, was feeling good.

"You real comfortable, Marshal?" he asked in his dry, jeering way.

The lawman gave no reply. Tolbert grinned. "Still not doing any talking, eh?

Well, you're smart. Best you save your breath all right. Come morning you'll be needing all you've got when you start swinging at the end of a rope."

Rye continued to be silent, causing some of the newfound joy in Tolbert to fade. He swore, shifted the sack of gold coins, taken from Gillespie's saddlebags, in his shirt a bit more to the back.

"Go right ahead, keep on being close-mouthed so folks'll think you're real brave. Won't count for anything when we string you up—and that's something I aim to enjoy. I'll be standing there laughing when they run that horse of yours out from under you and you feel that rope snapping your neck.

"And I'll be remembering that woman of yours, how pretty she was when I first had her and how she smelled—like lilacs—and how soft she was. She did exactly what I told her to do and never once did any complaining. You think about her, Marshal, and how I beat you then and how I've beat you again."

Rye barely stirred. Tolbert could see the man's pale, unblinking eyes fixed upon him. A surge of ungovernable rage—unusual for Jake Tolbert who always prided himself on never losing his composure—rocked the outlaw.

"Damn you—why don't you say something!" he shouted and, kicking out, drove a booted foot into the lawman's side.

"Hey—what's going on out there?" a voice called from the doorway of the saloon.

Tolbert, recovering quickly, pivoted. Raising a hand he waved reassuringly at the man—Sanderson, he thought it was.

"Just taking a look at our prisoner," Tolbert said. "Want to be sure he'll be here in the morning."

Sanderson laughed. "Hell, there ain't no chance of him getting loose. Tied them knots myself—me and Tennessee did . . . How long you been out here?"

Tolbert began to move slowly, indifferently toward the saloon. "A few minutes. Too damn warm inside."

"Well, you sure missed a humdinger of a scrap," Sanderson said, pulling back to allow Jake pass and enter the doorway. "Was a real stem-winder!"

"Heard some scuffling going on over there by the bar when I was leaving," Jake said. "Who was it and what was it all about?"

"Was your partner, Bone Enright. Him and some cowhand. They mixed it up a 'plenty. Was over one of the gals."

"Sounds like Bone, all right," Tolbert

commented with a shake of his head and moving on into the saloon sat down at one of the empty tables, saddlebags hung across his lap as before.

Jake would as soon no one had seen him outside, but his luck—just as it had been with cards the past few years—hadn't been good. He'd not fret about it, though. Sanderson had believed him when he'd said he went out to have a look at Rye. If the question came up, Enright would take Sanderson's word for it—but the question wouldn't come up unless Enright had ideas of claiming Gillespie's gold, too.

18

Rye drew up slowly, eyes turned to the source of the sound. Presently a figure emerged from the close-by brush. It was Pearly Joplin. The lawman scowled angrily.

"What the hell are you doing here? I left you back in Springerville with the parson and his family—"

"I couldn't stay," the girl replied.

Rye was shaking his head. "Sure shouldn't have come here. Things are a bit tight. How did you find me?"

"Didn't at first. This place being off the road like it is, I passed right on by. Later on, when I didn't come across your night camp, I decided you must have stopped and that I'd just somehow missed you. Started doubling back, saw the lights of this place, and guessed this is where you'd be. But I didn't expect to find you tied up like this. Who did it—the men you were after, Tolbert and Enright?''

Rye nodded, began to work at the cord binding his wrists with the knife. ''Along with three others just like them that they threw in with.''

Pearly glanced toward the saloon. ''Sounds like they're having a high old time in there. It got something to do with their plans for you?''

Rye grinned wryly. ''Everything. They're all set to hang me in the morning—but I don't aim to accommodate them.''

Pearly moved in closer to the lawman and laid her hands on his. ''Here, let me do that,'' she said.

Rye surrendered the knife and then murmured a low warning. A figure had appeared in the doorway of the saloon.

''Back in the brush—quick,'' the marshal whispered. ''It's Tolbert. Might come over here to have a look, be sure I'm still here.''

But Tolbert evidently had other things on his mind at the moment. Crossing the porch he descended to the hardpack and made his

177

way to the tethered horses. Rye watched as the outlaw moved in beside the chestnut, explored the right-hand saddlebag briefly, then circled the horse to get at the opposite pouch. The marshal realized then what Tolbert was doing; he was after Gillespie's bag of gold. Earlier the outlaw had apparently recognized his dead partner's saddlebags and was now searching through them in hopes of finding the fifteen thousand dollars in double eagles.

Rye's lips parted in a hard smile. Outlaws never changed. Tolbert was double-crossing Bone Enright, taking the bag of gold which he was certain to find and adding it to his own share. He would say nothing to Enright about it.

As Tolbert tucked the bag into his own saddlebags and hung them across his shoulder, he turned and started for the saloon. Midway he paused, changed course.

"Careful," Rye warned the girl softly. "He's coming over here."

Tolbert, swaggering broadly, came to a halt in front of the lawman.

"You real comfortable, Marshal?" he asked.

Rye made no reply, nor did he give Tolbert the satisfaction of making any answers when the outlaw taunted him about Beth or when Tolbert, angered by the stubborn silence the lawman maintained, kicked him brutally in the ribs.

In truth, it was all John Rye could do to keep his lips tight, to not lunge to his feet and hurl himself at the outlaw. Had he succeeded in freeing his hands as he had begun to do, in all likelihood he would have plunged his knife into the smirking, insulting outlaw's heart—and thereby broken the commitment he'd made to the law that he would bring Jake Tolbert in alive. Jaw set, grim, Rye weathered the pain and the snide words—and thanked his good fortune that his hands had not been free.

"Hey—what's going on out there?" a voice called from the saloon's entrance.

It was one of Enright's friends—the one named Sanderson and the one who had more or less run the kangaroo court trial.

"Just taking a look at our prisoner," Tolbert replied and then added something about only wanting to be sure the prisoner would be there when morning and the time for the hanging arrived.

Sanderson had scoffed at that, and Rye had a few bad moments when he thought the outlaw would come over and make certain the knots in the rope and cords binding him were secure. He'd have a hard time hiding the knife if such occurred, but luck was with him. Sanderson remained on the porch where he was joined by Tolbert. Rye caught snatches of their conversation—something about a fight that had taken place in the saloon and that Jake Tolbert had missed.

The lawman waited until he was certain the two outlaws were inside Jessup's and would not for some reason change their minds and return; then he turned to the girl, well hidden in the dense brush.

"Can come out—they're gone."

Pearly appeared from the shadows at once and wordlessly took the knife in her hands and as if only then realizing the urgent need for Rye to be free, quickly cut through the rawhide linking his wrists. Taking the sharp blade from her the marshal severed the cords that tied his ankles together and then, removing the rope from around his body, got to his feet. As an afterthought he picked up the lengths of rawhide cord, thrust them into a pocket for possible later use, and turned to the girl.

"I don't like the idea of you being here," he said, taking Pearly by the shoulders. "It's way too dangerous—but I thank you for it, anyway. It would've taken me most of the night to cut through that rawhide. Like to ask you one more favor."

Pearly pressed closer to him. "What is it?"

"Want you to get on your horse and head back to Springerville—get as far away from here as you can."

Pearly was shaking her head even before he had finished speaking. "No—I'm going to stay with you! If something bad happens, I want it to happen to me, too."

"That's a fool way to look at it," Rye snapped, angered.

"Maybe so, but that's how I want it."

The marshal swore quietly. "All right. I don't have time to argue with you— daylight's not far off. Stay if you've made up your mind, but be damn sure you keep out of the line of fire if it comes down to a shoot-out."

Pearly nodded, frowned. In the moonlight now filtering down through the branches and pine needles her face was a soft oval, and her skin looked as if it were made of some creamy, tan substance while her eyes appeared dark and lustrous.

"How can you do anything when there are so many of them in there?" she wondered, concern filling her voice. "There must be a dozen or more judging from the racket going on. Wouldn't it be better to go get help from somewhere?"

"Could use it for sure," Rye said, starting toward the horses. "But there's none around, so it's up to me to skin this cat."

"And me," Pearly said, hurrying to keep pace with his long stride. "What are you going to do first?"

"Get a gun. One of them took my forty-five. I've got a spare in my saddlebags. Rifle's there in the boot, too, unless one of them helped himself to it after they tied up the horses."

Reaching the chestnut Rye unbuckled the straps of the right-hand pouch. Delving into it he located the pistol he'd replaced a time back with a new model that had taken his fancy and drawing it out, tested its action. The heavy Colt, also a forty-five, worked perfectly, and seeing to a loading of fresh cartridges from the loops in his belt, Rye slid it into the holster.

"Rifle's here, too," he heard Pearly say.

The lawman nodded absently, his eyes on a window in the near wall of Jessup's. He'd have a look inside, see how matters were. Crossing quickly Rye made his way through the weeds and low brush growing against the building and removing his hat, looked through the dusty glassed opening.

Tolbert, Enright, Sanderson, Jessup, and two other men were gathered around a table engaged in a game of cards. He let his eyes move on. With the exception of one couple —a man and one of the saloon women who were at another table—everyone was gathered about the poker players looking on. Rye singled out Tennessee and Gabe Potter and fixed their positions in his mind— directly behind Sanderson.

One person was missing. He gave that deep thought and shortly realized it was the bartender. This brought a frown to his face that faded in the next moment when the man appeared, coming from a back room—one where supplies were kept, apparently, as he was carrying a box of something.

That completed his count, Rye thought with satisfaction. Earlier, while he was a prisoner inside the saloon undergoing the mock trial put on by the outlaws, he had made a head count of the men present, anticipating the need to have such information when—and if—he had an opportunity to go up against them. Stepping back from the side of the saloon, he faced Pearly.

"I'm going in after them," he said quietly. "They're all together. Be easy to handle them. If you want to help, get the horses and have them waiting in front."

"I know which one's yours," the girl said at once, "but Tolbert's and Enright's—"

Rye pointed out the gray Bone Enright rode and the black that was Tolbert's. "Best place to do the waiting will be at the other end of the porch. Darker there."

Pearly signified her understanding. The lawman smiled at her. "Get started. I'll wait until you're set then make my move."

The girl turned away and hurried to the horses. Rye returned to the window and for a time stood next to the square of yellow light again looking in, watching the play at the table, the couple who were off to one side, and the bartender, and then, once more taking a count and finding it unchanged, he made his way to the landing. Stepping up onto its weathered floor, Rye started for the saloon's entrance. He halted as the faint jingling of his spurs reached him. Taking a match from a shirt pocket, he broke it in half and wedged the portions against the rowels to silence them.

Rising, he moved again for the open doorway. Pearly would have had more than enough time by then to bring up the horses and have them ready, and hesitating no longer he continued. Reaching the entrance Rye tipped his hat forward over his eyes to shade them from any light coming from the chandeliers that might prove to be detrimental, and drawing and cocking his pistol, he stepped inside.

19

So intent were the patrons in Jessup's upon the card game that only the couple sitting beyond them noted Rye's abrupt entrance. The woman's eyes widened with surprise and the man, equally startled, lunged open-mouthed to his feet.

"It's him! The marshal!" he yelled in a raspy voice.

There was the quick clatter and scraping of chair legs and bootheels as everyone turned to look. Rye, standing well inside the doorway where he would not be taken unawares from the rear by some late arriving customer, coldly greeted the faces turned to him.

"On your feet—with your hands up!" he ordered.

There were a few moments of hesitation, and then several of the men who were seated rose and lifted their arms in unison with those standing who had been quick to comply. Rye, his attention centered mainly on Tolbert and Bone Enright, but with a wary eye on Sanderson and the others as well, motioned with his weapon.

"Get up against the wall—and face it!" he directed in the same cold, no-nonsense tone.

Again there was the scuffing of boots, the noise of chairs being pushed aside as the men moved to do as told. The lawman gestured again with his weapon, this time at the women who had drawn off in a group.

"Means you, too—"

The women, some shrugging indifferently, turned and started to take places with the line of men.

"You ain't telling me what to do!" one of the outlaws—Tennessee—shouted suddenly and pivoted, gun in hand.

Rye fired once. The bullet knocked the gunman back against the man who was standing next him. Tennessee hung there briefly, weapon falling from his hand, and then toppled forward. As the rebounding echoes in the room began to fade and coils of smoke drifted away from Rye, he moved slowly toward the men facing the wall.

"Don't want to kill any of you," he said, stepping near enough to the first man in the line to pluck the pistol from his holster and toss it into a corner, "but I will if you get in my way."

Sanderson, the second man in the silent row, half turned as the lawman removed his weapon and glanced at the dead man sprawled on the floor.

"Tennessee," he muttered. "That there was a friend of mine you put under. If I ever get the chance to even up for him—"

"Keep looking at the wall," Rye snapped, "or you'll be laying there beside him!"

Moving quickly along, the marshal disarmed the remaining men in the room, recovering his own pistol from Bone Enright who had apparently claimed it after the ambush on the trail. Thrusting the spare weapon he was using under his belt, he checked the load in the more familiar gun and finding the cylinder full, started to herd his captives, with the exception of Tolbert and Enright, toward the storeroom in the back. At that moment Rye saw Pearly Joplin.

The girl was standing a few steps behind him, holding his rifle cocked and leveled in the general direction of the outlaws. Her features were taut, and he could see the long gun wavering slightly in her hands. A mixture of anger and admiration shot through the lawman. Despite the fear and nervousness that gripped the girl she had chosen to enter the saloon and back his play although it would have been safer to stay outside with the horses as he had instructed her to do. As he caught her eye a ragged smile parted her lips. Rye nodded.

"Keep that gun on them till I tie up Enright and Tolbert," he said. "Then we'll lock the rest of them in the storeroom."

Pearly, evidently electing not to speak for fear a quaver in her voice would betray her inner feelings, merely moved in closer.

"Any one of them moves, shoot," Rye added as he drew from a pocket the rawhide cords that had earlier bound his own wrists and ankles.

Stepping in behind Jake Tolbert, he pulled the outlaw's arms down behind the back, and tied the man's hands together tightly. Tolbert uttered no sound during the process, but with Enright it was different.

"You ain't getting away with this!"

Enright declared as Rye secured his wrists in like manner. "Folks here are all friends of mine. You won't get a mile away before they come after me."

"They're welcome to try," the lawman said, drawing back.

He gave consideration to relieving the two outlaws of the gold they were carrying, but discarded the thought. Tolbert and Enright had made no show of their wealth for fear it would excite others in Jessup's and perhaps give them ideas. He'd best follow their cue and take the same precautions. Later on, when they were safely on the road, he would collect all of the double eagles and put them in one pair of the saddlebags where they would be easier to handle.

Grasping the muttering Enright by a shoulder, Rye whirled the outlaw about and sat him down in a nearby chair. Following the same procedure with the glowering but silent Tolbert, the lawman beckoned to the girl.

"Keep your gun on these two now. I'll take care of the others," he said and once again moved to put the remaining men and the women in Jessup's storeroom.

They turned sullenly at his direction, reluctantly crossed the floor to the rear of the saloon. Opening the door Rye glanced in, saw that the room was small and that it had no outside entrance but only a small window high in the wall for light. It would serve the purpose, but certainly not for long; it would take very little to break down the door.

The men and women filed in angry and cursing, Sanderson vowing revenge. Jessup also voiced dire threats along with shrill protests from the women. Rye turned a deaf ear to it all, and when the last of the group—Gabe Potter—was inside, he closed the door. There was no way of locking it, so to hold the panel secure, the lawman dragged a chair up and wedged it under the knob. That would secure the door for awhile, at least.

"Stay put in there for fifteen minutes," he said, standing close to the thin, wooden panel so that he could be heard. "Aim to be busy out here for a bit, and I don't want anybody getting in my way."

"Go to hell," a muffled voice replied from within the crowded storeroom.

The marshal, holstering his weapon, quickly rejoined Pearly and the two outlaws. "On your feet," he ordered, grasping Enright by the arm and pulling him upright. "Got the horses waiting outside."

"The hell with you!" Enright snarled. "You want me, you'll have to tote me—"

Rye drew his pistol. In a swift move he clubbed the outlaw solidly on the side of the head. Enright groaned and sank back onto the chair. Again Rye seized him by an arm, yanked him to his feet, and sent him stumbling toward the saloon's entrance.

"How about you?" he demanded in a savage tone to Tolbert. "You need a little help, too?"

Jake, dark eyes alive with hate, drew himself up and followed Enright to the exit. At that moment someone in the storeroom began to kick and hammer on the door in an effort to force it open. Rye raised his pistol and, aiming at a spot in the wall inches above the door facing, sent a bullet smashing into the dry wood. All efforts to break out of the room ceased instantly.

With Pearly keeping the rifle leveled on Tolbert and Bone Enright, Rye gathered up the outlaws' saddlebags and hurried to catch up. Reaching the porch he glanced about, saw the horses tied to a post at its end, and, again prodding the men to move faster, got them to their mounts and into the saddle.

"How am I going to ride with my hands tied behind me like this?" Enright complained. "Ain't right making a man do—"

"You'll manage," Rye cut in and looked at Tolbert to see if he was set and ready to go.

Tolbert met his glance, spat. "You'll never get me back to Prescott," he said coolly.

"Don't bet on that," the lawman replied and taking the reins of Enright's horse, tied them to a ring on the skirt of Tolbert's saddle. Then holding to the lines of Tolbert's black, he swung onto the chestnut. Leading the outlaws' horses in such manner would make for slow going, but that, too, he would change once they were well away from Jessup's and had the time to make better arrangements.

A crash sounded in the saloon, followed by yells. Rye swore. The storeroom door had apparently given way. Sanderson and the others would be coming out.

The lawman glanced ahead. The main road that would take them back to Springerville, Show Low, and on to Prescott lay on the far side of Jessup's. To reach it meant leading his party past the saloon's entrance. He'd never make it. By the time he could draw opposite the door, all of the men would have recovered their weapons and be in a position to open up on him.

He had but one choice—take the trail that led into the opposite direction, one that headed into the higher hills, now taking towering shape in the first cold light of early morning.

"That way!" he shouted at the girl, pointing. "We'll double back later."

Pearly wheeled her horse about wordlessly, raked him with her spurs, and sent him loping up the trail. Rye, holding tight to the reins of Tolbert's black with one hand, drew his gun. Twisting about, he fired two quick shots in the direction of the saloon's doorway and then, also making use of his rowels, followed the girl.

20

They reached the first stand of trees and thick brush in only moments. Rye, looking back over a shoulder, saw one of the outlaws, Gabe Potter, appear in the rectangle of light that was the doorway of the saloon. The man was crouched, uncertain of the exact whereabouts of Rye. The lawman snapped a shot at Potter, saw him duck back inside.

Reloading as the horses hurried along, Rye took note of the trail. It was one not too well used, he saw, and, as he'd noticed earlier, appeared to lead into the high mountain country that lay north of the main road. He had no idea where the path might eventually take him and his party—probably to some small settlement, he reckoned. But it didn't matter. He'd had no choice but to follow it, as it would have been foolhardy to try and cross in front of Jessup's. Later, when they were in the clear, he'd circle back, bypass the saloon by several miles, and rejoin the main road somewhere between where they now were and Springerville.

The lawman shifted his attention to the outlaws. Both were leaning back in their saddles, doing their utmost to keep from falling off their mounts. With hands tied behind them it was a difficult task, Rye knew, but as was his way, he wasted no sympathy on them.

They were outlaws, killers, and as such deserved no more consideration than they'd given the persons they had brutally murdered. But he guessed he'd have to make some changes; it would be a long trip back to Prescott and to force Tolbert and Enright to continue riding as they were would slow the pace too much. He'd figure out another arrangement that would keep the two men securely in hand but not hinder their traveling.

Rye slowed and pulled off to one side. As Tolbert's black drew abreast, Rye looped the reins back over the horse's bobbing head and hooked them about the saddle horn. Tolbert glared at him from beneath the brim of his hat.

"Don't get any ideas," Rye warned and turning to Enright added: "Goes for you, too. Either one of you tries to leave your saddle, I'll blow your head off. I'd as soon take you in hanging across that horse as riding him. Be a hell of a lot easier."

"You won't do that," Tolbert countered in a low voice. "I expect you've got strict orders to bring me in alive."

"Alive, maybe," the lawman said, a hard grin on his lips, "but not necessarily good as new. Nothing says I can't shoot your legs out from under you or bust both your arms and say you tried getting away from me."

Tolbert had no answer for that. Enright was also quiet but only for a few moments. Then, his voice uneven as he struggled to hold his seat in the saddle while the horses trotted steadily on, he swore vividly and spoke out.

"When the hell you going to untie my hands? Trying to stay aboard this nag hog-tied like this—I—"

"You'll stand it for a while," Rye said, dropping farther back to where he was behind Enright and his gray again.

They were moving well. Pearly, some yards in the lead, was setting the pace and the pattern for the others' horses, which were following along in line just as Rye had hoped. Allowing Enright to draw ahead a few strides, the lawman halted, turned, and faced their back trail.

He could hear faint shouting. It could only mean that pursuit by the friends of Tolbert and Enright had gotten underway. His last shot, which had driven Gabe Potter back into the saloon, and the time it had then taken for him and the others to get to their horses had delayed the outlaws considerably; but they would be coming on fast now and moving at a much better pace than he and his party.

But he did have a fair lead, Rye thought as he came about and got back in line, and if he could manage to get off a few shots at his pursuers when they first came into sight, there was the chance he could hold them off until he could reach a place where a stand could be made. Gabe Potter, Sanderson, and the others, discouraged by their inability to rescue Tolbert and Enright, might then give it up and turn back.

The marshal didn't know how strong the

friendship existing between his two prisoners and the outlaws in the oncoming party might be. Certainly no one appeared to be on good terms with Tolbert except Bone Enright. Indeed, it seemed to Rye that just the opposite was the fact; Jake had no use for them, and they had none for him.

With Bone Enright it was different. He evidently was well acquainted with Sanderson, Potter, and the gunman Tennessee, who was now out of the picture, and they with Jessup and three or four of the men in the saloon. But just how faithful any of them would be when it came to facing bullets on Enright's behalf was hard to say. Outlaws, Rye had learned from experience, were not overly burdened with loyalty for one another.

The horses were slowing, Rye noticed. The trail had become not only steeper but rougher and showed less use. Forging on ahead to where he was alongside Tolbert's black, Rye slapped the horse sharply on the rump to quicken its pace and then applied the same treatment to Enright's gray, after which he again dropped behind to where he could listen and watch.

An hour later, with the sun now well up in the clear blue of a spotless sky, there was still no sign of the riders that Rye was certain were still coming on. They should have at least come into view along the trail somewhere by then, he reasoned, and the fact they had not puzzled and disturbed him.

Around noon, as they were deep into the mountainous country, John Rye found the answer. He had twice more fallen back to look for the outlaws. He had just halted when four riders broke into view a half mile or so in the distance, too far for definite identification but he thought he recognized Sanderson and Potter. They were coming on slow and easy, seemingly in no great hurry to overtake him and their friends.

The lawman's mouth tightened as he glanced about at the steep, rocky slopes on either side of him. The walls were much closer now than they had been an hour earlier, which could only mean one thing; they were riding into a box canyon—a dead end.

That explained the lack of haste on the part of Sanderson and the others; they knew he could go only so far with Tolbert and Enright, that he eventually would be compelled to halt, and, no doubt being well acquainted with the particular area, anticipated no trouble in rescuing their two friends.

Back in the line Rye realized his party's horses were moving much slower as the trail had become more difficult. The ragged, brush-covered walls of the canyon were but a few yards to either side, and here and there he spotted dark holes, like gaping mouths, with mounds of lighter earth below them—evidence of one-time mining activity.

"We sure ain't going nowhere up here," Enright said, his skin shining with sweat. There was a note of triumph in his voice. "You're heading right into a box canyon. Only thing you can do is turn around and go back out the way we come."

Pearly Joplin, hearing the outlaw's words, slowed and looked inquiringly at Rye. The heat was laying its mark on her, too. There were patches of moisture on her tanned face, and she had removed her small-brimmed man's hat in search of coolness.

The lawman shook his head at her silent question. "Keep going—far as you can."

Pearly resumed the lifting trail. Bone Enright half turned, grinned at Rye. "I'm thinking the Doomsday Marshal's come to a doomsday canyon—leastwise his," he said.

The lawman, ignoring Enright's snide

comment, was looking ahead, beyond Pearly Joplin and her horse. The dark entrance to one of the mine shafts lay just off the trail a short distance farther on.

"Pearly, head for that," he called, catching the girl's attention, and pointing.

She nodded her understanding and a quarter-hour later swung off the now indefinite trail and led the party up to a small, level clearing in front of the mine opening.

Rye dismounted at once and, waiting until the girl was also on the ground, pulled Tolbert and Enright off their saddles. The mine shaft had caved in many years ago, apparently, for a tangle of weeds now covered the jumbled pile of rocks and earth blocking the entrance. This made the place ideal for what the marshal had in mind.

"Sit down over there," Rye ordered and pushed the outlaws toward the shaft.

Tolbert as usual made no comment and maintained his sullen, deadly silence. Enright, stumbling, swore loudly but he made no effort to do anything other than what he had been told. Both were sweating freely in the hot sunshine, and their clothing showed dark in many places.

Rye, taking the horses off to one side, tied

them to the sagging remainder of a hitchrack and then returned to where Pearly was staring off down the slope at the quartette of riders advancing slowly up the trail. Taking the rifle from her he jacked a cartridge into its chamber.

"Too far to do any damage," he said, aiming slightly above the heads of the riders, "but we might as well let them know we're here and they best take care."

The bullet dug into the trail ahead of the outlaws, and set echoes to rocking back and forth in the narrow canyon. The outlaws came to a stop. They remained in the saddle for moments while they talked over the situation and then all dismounted and, picketing their mounts, drew off to the side and settled down.

The girl turned to Rye. "What do we do now?"

"Keep an eye on them and wait," he replied, glancing at the slope rising above them. "Doubt there's any way out of here other than the trail, but I'll have a look . . . First off, though, I've got a little chore to take care of."

Wheeling, he crossed to where the outlaws were sitting. Halting in front of Tolbert he reached down and jerked open the man's shirt, revealing the money belt that encircled his waist. Releasing the buckle, Rye pulled it free.

"This isn't all of the money," he said and pulling the outlaw to his feet, went through his pockets and collected the rest of the double eagles.

Moving then to Enright, Rye opened his shirt, found a similar belt packed with gold coins and after taking possession of it, relieved the second outlaw of the coins he, too, had distributed in his pockets. Finished, the lawman moved toward the horses, paused.

"Expect you'd like to know this, Bone," he said. "While you were in Jessup's scrapping with that cowhand, your partner went outside and helped himself to the sack of double eagles that belonged to Gillespie I was packing. I don't think he figured to split it with you."

Enright whirled to Tolbert, features knotted with anger. "You—you lousy double-crossing sonofabitch!" he exploded. "Knew all along I should've never teamed up with a trigger-happy looney like you!"

Rye smiled as he reached the horses. Taking the saddlebags that had belonged to Gillespie, he dumped their contents onto the ground and placed the money belts and loose coins inside them. Going then to Tolbert's horse, he opened the pouch on the outlaw's saddle and obtained the bag of double eagles that had been Gillespie's. In so doing his fingers felt another bag, a smaller one containing coins. Opening it he saw it was more of the bank's money, a surplus no doubt that Tolbert was unable to carry on his person.

Adding the two sacks to the money he had in Gillespie's saddlebags, Rye moved on to Enright's gray gelding. Likely he had been forced to do the same with the coins he found he couldn't carry. Searching the pouches Rye came up with a third sack with about the same number of double eagles in it as were in that of Tolbert's. Dropping it in Gillespie's saddlebags, Rye cinched the straps down tight and then attached the pouches securely to his own saddle. A feeling of satisfaction was running through him; he had the bank's money—all of it, he was certain —in his possession now. The only thing that was left to do was get the two men who had murdered for it back to face the law.

Coming about and smiling slightly as he passed the quarreling outlaws, the marshal returned to the edge of the clearing where he joined Pearly Joplin as she kept watch on the four men down the trail.

As Rye had suspected, there was no other way out of the box canyon, which ended, he also discovered, a short distance farther on against the base of a sheer palisade.

"That means we'll have to fight our way out of here," the girl said when he returned and sat down beside her at the edge of the small flat.

He smiled at the resolution in her voice. "Maybe."

"What else can we do?"

"Wait for dark—like that bunch down the slope is doing."

"Then what? Won't we have to fight—keep them from—"

"We won't try holding them off—we'll be gone by the time they make it to this flat," Rye said, rising. "I've got to get a few things set. Keep an eye on them, and if they move, sing out."

Pearly nodded. "Is there anything else I can do?"

"No, just watch them—"

Crossing to the horses Rye took the coil of rope hanging from the saddle of the one the girl was riding. Shaking out the loops, he cut off two lengths fifteen feet or so long and laid them near the horses the outlaws were riding.

Turning then to his own mount, the lawman rummaged about in his saddlebags for some cloth, came up with an old, well-worn shirt. Tearing two strips from it he tucked them into a hip pocket and crossed to where Tolbert and Enright were watching him in silence. Halting before them, Rye called to the girl.

"I'm going to untie their hands," he said. "Keep your rifle on them till I'm done."

Releasing Enright first, he allowed the outlaw a few minutes to stretch his muscles and then linked the man's hands together again—this time in front of instead of behind his back. Ignoring Enright's steady complaining, he followed a similar plan with Tolbert.

When it was done, Enright said: "Just wasting your time, Marshal—doing a lot of sweating for nothing. Friends of mine'll be up here before you know it and cut me loose. And when they do, I aim to—"

"You want some water?" Rye cut in.

Bone nodded, and getting his canteen, the lawman stood by while Enright held the metal container to his lips and satisfied his thirst.

"What about you?" Rye asked then, taking the canteen and facing Tolbert.

Jake nodded slightly, accepted the container, and had several swallows of the tepid water, all the while keeping his agate-hard, dark eyes fixed on the lawman. There was no need for him to speak; his hatred of Rye was so intense that it burned like a steady, almost visible flame within him. Rye had upset the new world he had envisioned for himself, a life of wealth and ease among persons of quality; and while he had yet to play his hole card ace, the treatment he was being accorded cut him to the core.

But his seething hate was no fiercer than John Rye's. Each time the marshal looked at Tolbert an overwhelming desire swept through him to throw himself upon the outlaw, batter his smirking face to a bloody pulp, and then finish the job once and for all with his six-gun. But satisfaction was never to be his. The law had ranking priority on the killer and as such had to be honored.

"Turn around—back to back," the lawman ordered, and when that was done Rye took what remained of the rope he'd cut and bound the two men together.

"What're you doing this for?" Enright demanded.

"Just don't want you up and wandering about," the marshal replied.

His actual intent was to keep the outlaws from untying the rawhide cord that bound their wrists now that their hands were accessible to one another. He had made the change, not for the convenience and comfort of the outlaws, but in order for them to stay on their horses when, and if, escape developed into a fast race.

"Ain't there nothing to eat?" Enright complained as Rye moved off.

"Nothing," the lawman answered. "I'll feed you later tonight after we've made camp."

Tolbert saw fit to again break his silence. "You won't live that long," he said with an irritating laugh. "You'll be dead and in hell before you ever get out of this canyon."

"Then we'll all be there together," Rye said dryly and continued on his way.

He spent another half hour dragging up wood for a fire, after which he took his place beside the girl. The outlaws had not changed from their original positions, he saw.

"When it gets dark I'm going to head

back down the trail with Tolbert and Enright," he said, keeping his voice low. "Aim to have them tied to their saddles, and gagged so they can't sing out."

Pearly frowned, and her eyes filled with concern. "Won't you run into those men down there? There's four of—"

"I figure they'll be coming up the trail. I figure to find a wide place where I can pull off and sit tight until they've passed by. Brush is thick, and it'll be dark. Got one big worry, however."

"What's that?"

"You. I won't risk you being with me. If something goes wrong, it means a shoot-out—and you could get hurt."

"I could help. There'd be two of us—"

"Against them you'd only get yourself killed. What I want you to do is go on up the canyon a piece when I leave and find yourself a good place to wait. I'm going to sucker that bunch up to the flat with a fire. When they see I've pulled out with their friends, they'll head back down the trail after me. You stay put for awhile—until you're sure they're gone—then come on down."

"Where'll I meet you?" Pearly asked, after she had given the plan consideration.

"I'll be on the road to Springerville after

I've shaken that bunch, got them off my heels."

"Then how will I find you?"

"You just head for Springerville—I'll be watching for you."

21

Darkness came early on the mountain because of a bank of heavy, rain-filled clouds hanging low over the western horizon. It was to Rye's liking. He deemed it important that he be on the way down the trail with the outlaws by the time night closed in.

"On your feet," he ordered, gesturing with his pistol at Enright and Tolbert. "Want you on your horses," he added, removing the rope that pinned them together.

Tolbert, casting a side glance at Pearly Joplin standing to one side with the rifle leveled, came slowly erect and started for the hitchrack. Enright, muttering curses and threats, followed suit. With their hands now in front of them, both were able to grasp the horn and swing up into the saddle without assistance. Rye, noting the sly, meaningful look Enright gave Tolbert as he settled onto his gray horse, smiled and drawing another strip of rawhide from his pocket, stepped in close to the man.

"Keep your hands on the saddle horn," he directed.

Enright complied frowningly. The lawman quickly grasped the man's locked-together wrists, pressed them against the metal horn, and running the rawhide through the fork, tied the outlaw securely to the saddle.

Enright, cursing, struggled briefly and then slumped. "You're doing all this for nothing," he said in a voice ragged with anger. "You ain't going to get away from the boys. They're down there just waiting for you."

Rye, only half listening, was busy linking Jake Tolbert to the saddle of his black. The outlaw had nothing to say, but when the lawman proceeded to the next step he had planned to keep his prisoners safe—connecting the feet of each man by running a length of rope under the belly of his horse and knotting each end around the rider's ankles like a cinch—Tolbert found his voice.

"This isn't right! You're not supposed to treat a man this way—it's cruel."

The marshal, moving to where Enright sat on his horse, looked back at Tolbert, his face dark with anger. "Who the hell are you to talk about cruelty?" he snarled. "It's you that's made a habit of it! I'm hoping you'll be miserable every mile of the way back to Prescott."

"Told you before, you'll never get me there," Tolbert said evenly.

"And I told you not to make any bets," Rye snapped, begining to tie Bone Enright's feet together as he had done Tolbert's.

"Don't do no worrying about it, Jake," Enright said confidently. "We won't be putting up with this for long. Ira and the boys'll take care of this tin star." Bone paused briefly. "And when they do, I'll be expecting my half of Gillespie's gold."

Tolbert shrugged. "Sure. Can settle that once we get out of here."

"That won't be long," Enright said and glanced down the slope. A moment later he added: "I'm kind of sorry you messed around with his woman. Sure has made him mean, meaner'n usual, anyway."

"The hell with him," Tolbert said flatly, and then as Rye, using a nearby rock to stand on, drew a strip of cloth cross his mouth and knotted it tightly in place, he began to struggle and try to pull away.

Rye, ignoring the outlaw, moved then to Enright. He also endeavored to draw back and avoid the gag, but the rope that bound his legs to his horse and the cord connecting him to the saddlehorn permitted but little movement.

"You ain't gagging me!" he shouted.

For answer Rye slapped him sharply. The outlaw, slightly stunned, drew up stiffly, and the lawman, taking advantage of the moment, quickly tied the cloth in place.

Pearly, watching it all in silence until Rye had finished, said, "Will they have to ride like that all the way to Prescott?"

The lawman crossed to where he had piled wood for a fire. Directly in front of it, so the flames would create silhouettes visible to anyone coming up the trail, were two figures made by weeds stuffed into a pair of shirts found among Gillespie's discarded possessions and mounted on sticks driven into the ground. From a distance they would appear to be two persons hunched before the fire.

"That'll be up to them," Rye said, finally

215

answering the girl's question.

Rye glanced about. It was full dark. He'd best be starting, feeling that it was important for him to have his prisoners fairly well down the trail before Sanderson and his three friends began the climb. The outlaws would probably stay together, Rye figured, until they were within fifty yards or so of the mine shaft and then would split up and approach the flat from different points.

"You know what you're to do?" the marshal said to Pearly as he struck a match and thrust it into a pile of dry wood.

"Wait until those men are gone, then follow—"

Rye stepped back as the flames began to rise. "Watch yourself. Don't follow too close."

Pearly looked off down the canyon in the direction of the outlaws. It was now too dark to tell if they were still there or had moved.

"I—I wish I could just go with you—"

"Better this way," Rye replied and crossed to the hitchrack.

Freeing the reins of each horse, the lawman fastened the lines of Enright's gray to a ring in Tolbert's saddle, as before. Then taking up the leathers of Tolbert's black, he swung onto the chestnut. Pearly stepped in close and began to slide the rifle into its boot.

"Keep it," Rye said, "and don't be scared to use it if need be." As the girl nodded and pulled back, he added: "See you later on the road to Springerville."

Pulling away, Rye headed down the slope for the trail, leading the horses of Tolbert and Enright closely. He disliked leaving Pearly Joplin there on her own, but he knew it was the only thing he could do. As always with John Rye, the needs of the law came first, and having the girl with him could complicate his getting his prisoners and himself out of the trap he'd blundered into—a situation he would not permit. Besides, following his instructions, she'd undoubtedly be much safer.

Reaching the trail, Rye paused to listen. He could hear nothing but the clicking of night insects and the far-off hooting of an owl. Roweling the chestnut lightly, he continued on, raking his memory as he tried to recall where the canyon opened up more and would allow him to pull off, and, screened by dense brush, let Sanderson and the men with him pass.

Tension began to build within the lawman as he pressed on. He was drawing nearer the point where he had seen the outlaws waiting, and no suitable place to turn off had appeared. Sanderson and the others would have begun their approach by then, he was certain.

The faint click of metal on rock came to Rye. A horseshoe striking rock—he recognized the sound instantly. The outlaws were just ahead of him. No longer searching for an ideal spot in which to hide, Rye turned off the trail at once and led his prisoners as deep as possible into the brush, scrub trees, and rocks and halted. They were not far from the trail, but it would have to do. Drawing his pistol, he glanced at Tolbert and Enright.

"One sound out of you or your horses, and I'll crack your skull with this," he said in a whisper.

Rye could barely see the two outlaws' features in the half light but knew they understood. If either had been entertaining thoughts of stirring about or forcing their mounts to make a noise, he would think twice about it now. The lawman had already demonstrated to Bone Enright that he was not averse to using his forty-five as a club.

Abruptly Sanderson and the others were nearby. Rye could not see them because of the increasing cloudiness of the night and the thick brush, but he could hear the quiet thud of their horses' hoofs. The men were not talking, evidently fearing their voices might carry and be heard by him—supposedly still up on the flat.

The marshal allowed them to pass, and when he could no longer hear their movements, he led the way quietly back to the trail. Continuing on down the canyon, Rye held the horses to a fast walk until he was near its mouth and then broke them into a good lope—taking care to swing wide of Jessup's, which proved to be well lighted and attended, just as it had been the previous night.

Rye and his prisoners reached the main road shortly after that, and turning west, the marshal put the horses to a steady lope. There were muffled words of protest from the outlaws, both hoping at least to get their gags removed, but it was a full hour later, after being certain he could hear no sounds of pursuit, that Rye halted and untied the cloths.

"Ain't hardly been able to breathe," Enright grumbled. "Sure took your time taking them rags off."

"It'll go right back on if you keep

shooting off your mouth," Rye, impatient, snapped, eyes again on the trail behind them.

"What about untying my hands?" Enright continued. "Riding all trussed up like this is killing me."

The lawman smiled slightly, stuffed the gags into a pocket and looked at Tolbert. "It killing you, too?"

Jake spat into the grass alongside the road. "The hell with you," he muttered,

The lawman's grin widened, and taking up the reins of the chestnut, he mounted and resumed the trail.

He wasn't certain in his mind if Sanderson and the men with him would continue their efforts to take Tolbert and Bone Enright away from him or not. They had already experienced considerable trouble and gotten nowhere, Now tired, no doubt hungry, and thinking of the delights that could be had at Jessup's, they might call it off. Rye hoped so. He was feeling the need of food and rest himself.

But he pressed on, not pushing the horses hard but keeping them at a good, ground-covering pace until daylight. At that point he swung off the road at a placc where brush and trees grew close to the shoulder, and a lengthy view of his back trail was offered.

"You letting us climb down?" Enright asked as Rye stepped from his saddle.

The lawman made no reply, but once the chestnut was picketed he returned to his prisoners. Untying the rope from the ankles of each and releasing the strips of leather that pinned their hands to the saddlehorns, he allowed them to dismount and led them to a close-by pine and attached them to it. Such would allow them to move about in a small area.

"Keep apart," he warned, going into his saddlebags for coffee, what food he had, and the utensils necessary to prepare a quick meal. "I see you together—maybe trying to get that cord off your wrists—I'll tie your hands behind you again and let them stay that way till we get to Prescott."

Building a small fire, Rye put water on to boil for coffee and broke out the dried meat and hard biscuits that were to be the meal. Enright grumbled his displeasure as he made away with his share. Tolbert, as usual, remained closemouthed and sullen, but being hungry, ate all that was offered him.

A little more than an hour later the quick beat of a galloping horse came to them. Immediately Enright leaped to his feet, a wide grin on his bewhiskered face.

"Told you, didn't I?" he shouted. "Said my friends would be coming! Mister marshal, you best hunt yourself a hole 'cause you're sure in for a bad time!"

Rye, eyes fixed on a bend in the trail a short distance away, watched grimly. It sounded like a single horse to him, not four as the outlaw was predicting, but he could not be sure. Pistol in hand, he waited.

"Aw, hell—it's that woman!"

Enright's voice sagged as he caught sight of the rider rounding the bend. Rye, seeing Pearly Joplin at the same instant as the outlaw, allowed his shoulders to relent. Tension running from him, he holstered his gun and stepped out of the brush to intercept the girl. He caught her attention at once, and leaving the road, she swung into the camp.

"I was afraid I'd missed you," she said, giving Rye her bright smile as she dismounted. There was relief in her voice.

"I was watching for you," the lawman assured her. "Have any trouble?"

"No—none. Everything went just like you said it would."

"What about Sanderson and the others?" Rye asked. "Figured they'd be following us."

Pearly shook her head and, moving to the fire, filled one of the empty cups with coffee.

Rye, realizing the girl must also be hungry, provided her with a portion of the meat and biscuits.

"Ain't they coming?" Enright asked, his tone filled with doubt and disappointment.

"I came on down the trail after they left," Pearly said, directing her words to Rye. "When I got to that saloon—"

"Jessup's—"

"They were standing out in front talking to some other men. I was in the brush off to the side but I wasn't close enough to hear what they were saying. After a bit they all went inside. I hung around for a little while, then rode in to where I could see what they were doing. Three of them were at the bar drinking, the other one was at one of the tables, playing cards."

"That don't mean nothing," Enright declared. "Was all just having a drink and resting a bit. They'll be coming."

"They might, but I wouldn't bank on it," Rye said and turned to see if the girl needed any more to satisfy her hunger. Bone Enright's friends were running true to form insofar as outlaws were concerned; they would help, maybe, if it was convenient, and there wasn't too much risk involved.

It was around dark a day later when they

223

reached Springerville. They had seen no more of Sanderson and the other outlaws, but had lost some time in circling past the area where, at Enright's admission, Tolbert had killed the two Indians.

"I know them redskins!" Enright had said, fear showing plainly in his eyes. "They'll be hunting for us. Was Jake that done the killing, but I was with him, so they'll be looking to peg me out on an anthill, too."

To John Rye it was another painful twist of irony, once more he was obliged to protect a man he hated and who deserved the worst that could be meted out to him by people he had wronged. But as before, the lawman put personal feelings aside, and did what was expected of him.

Rye took his prisoners direct to the town marshal's office. Although the pair had given him no problems, he felt the need to get them off his hands for a few hours so that he might relax.

Ben Winters came out of his quarters, hat on the back of his head, a grin on his face.

"See you got them! Good! Sure would like to put them on trial right here and now for what they done to the Radmons—"

"Can understand that, but they belong to

Prescott," Rye said, leaving his saddle. "They'll hang there—you can figure on it . . . . Chance I can use your jail for the night?"

"Welcome to it," Winters said, glancing at Pearly—"Was wondering what happened to you"—and then brought his attention back to Rye. "While I'm thinking of it, I looked up them two jaspers you brought in the other day. Rewards on both of them—two-fifty on one, a thousand on the other. I don't have the money to pay off here but I'll give you vouchers and you can collect from the sheriff when you get to Prescott."

"Obliged to you," Rye said, taking the folded slips of paper Winters offered him. Tucking them into a pocket, he untied the ropes that held the outlaws to their horses and released the cords binding them to their saddle horns. Gun in hand, he then stepped back. Pearly, off her mount and rifle ready, moved in beside him.

"Climb down," Rye ordered when the outlaws made no effort to dismount, "unless you aim to spend the night up there."

Bone Enright shook his head. "Handy as you are with that hogleg, I ain't doing nothing till you tell me to," he said, and swung off his gray.

Tolbert was apparently of the same conviction. Rye watched both men narrowly as they left their horses, each with wrists still bound, and then the lawman, backed by Pearly and Ben Winters, escorted the outlaws into separate cells in the jail.

"We'll be riding out at first light," he advised the pair as they sank wearily onto the bunks provided for prisoners. "Be the same arrangement."

Enright groaned. Then: "What about some feed?" he wondered in his whining, complaining way. "I ain't had a square meal in weeks."

"You'll get supper later on," Rye answered and turned to Winters. "I'll feed them myself—I don't want anybody around them but me."

The town marshal nodded. "Sure thing, whatever you say. Where'll you be in case I need you?"

"I'm taking the lady to the hotel and getting her a room and another one for myself. After that I'll be at the general store laying in a supply of trail grub. You can do me a favor by lining up a pack horse for me."

"Sure thing—"

"One more thing—might keep your eye peeled on the road east for some of Enright's friends. Be two or maybe four in the party. Not sure they followed us, but they might've."

"Got any names? Could be wanted—"

"Sanderson and Potter—that'd be two of them. Can't tell you anything about the others."

Winters nodded. "I'll be watching."

22

"That will be Prescott," Rye said when days later they broke out onto a round-topped ridge and looked down on the settlement nestled in a hollow of the high, thickly forested mountains.

Enright swore quietly. "Sure never figured to be looking ahead to going to jail—but anything'll beat having to ride like we've been doing," he said heavily.

Rye shrugged indifferently. He had not changed the way he had kept his prisoners under control—hands tied to their saddle horns, feet linked together under their horses' bellies—and it had worked. He had successfully brought Tolbert and Enright

228

back, without any problems to speak of, to the town where they would be tried and sentenced for the crimes they had committed.

"I'll be glad to get there, too," Pearly said. She was riding beside the marshal on the well-traveled road. "It seems months since we left Springerville."

"Been a long ride," the lawman agreed. Tolbert, slumped in his hull, and Bone Enright, sitting to one side in his as he sought to relieve his aching muscles, were ahead of them. "You still figure you'd like to be a school teacher, Pearly?"

The girl's shoulders stirred. Taking a bandanna from a pocket she brushed at the moisture on her face,

"Yes, but there's not much use planning on it. I need more schooling myself—and that takes money." She paused, brought up the subject she had apparently hoped to discuss earlier in the journey. "John, before we go any farther—have you thought any more about us—about me?"

"Some—"

She looked at him intently. "Do I mean anything to you?"

Rye turned to the girl. "You could if I'd allow you to—but that's something I'll never let happen—not with you or any other woman—"

"Why not? I don't think I—"

"There's nothing I can give a wife but loneliness and worry. I've been though a marriage once, put both my wife and me into hell—and one time is enough."

Pearly studied him closely, her features soft, eyes filled with a gentleness. She was having a better understanding of this stiff-backed, letter-of-the-law marshal, was realizing what drove him so recklessly and fiercely. But she was not one to give up hope.

"I think it could be different with us," she said quietly.

"Doubt it. Better for you to go your way while I go mine. That'll be the best thing. One day a man will come along who'll give you what you deserve in this life, and make you happy."

Pearly's shoulders stirred. "I'm afraid you've spoiled me for any other man."

"Nonsense. The right man will come along."

The girl gave no response, and a short time later they rode into the settlement and were drawing to a stop in front of the sheriff's office.

"This won't take long," Rye said to her as

he came off his horse. "Stay where you are."

A brisk young man wearing a deputy's star came out of the office. He glanced at Pearly appreciatively as he stuck out his hand to Rye.

"Good to see you again, Marshal. See you got the killers—at least two of them."

"Had to shoot the third one," Rye said, releasing Gillespie's saddlebags and handing them to the lawman. "Here's the bank's money. All there, I think. The sheriff around, Tom?"

"Nope. Went to Tucson. Ain't looking for him back till the end of the week. Left me in charge."

A second deputy had come from the sheriff's office, and several persons attracted by the sight of the two prisoners sitting motionless on their horses had edged in for a closer look.

Rye, crossing to Tolbert, removed the rope that linked the outlaw's feet and the cord that held him to his saddle. Continuing on to Bone Enright, he freed him also.

"They're all yours," he said to the deputy. "Best you watch them close."

Tom, hanging the saddlebags containing the double eagles over his shoulder, said,

"Can bet we will. Mason, take the prisoners inside and lock them up."

The deputy who had just appeared stepped forward and motioned for the outlaws to dismount. Rye, watching the procedure from a corner of an eye, produced the reward vouchers given to him by Ben Winters in Springerville.

"Like to have the cash for these," he said, handing the slips to the deputy. "Comes to twelve hundred and fifty dollars."

"Sure thing," Tom said, reading the vouchers. " 'For Rube Henry, one thousand dollars. For Anson Smith, two hundred and fifty.' Can't give you cash, Marshal—that ain't the way we do it. I give you a draft and you take it over to the bank and cash it."

"Good enough," Rye said, turning about completely so that he could face Tolbert and Enright and the deputy who had taken charge of them. "Make the draft out to Miss Pearly Joplin. Was her that fixed it so's I could nail that pair. She's going to be a schoolteacher."

"That the lady there?" Tom asked, looking at the girl now coming off her horse, surprise widening her eyes.

"That's her," Rye replied. "What did you say that deputy's name was?"

"Mason—Mason Hillerman," Tom said, smiling at Pearly. "Come on inside with me, young lady, and I'll make out your draft."

"Hillerman," Rye warned, seeing the deputy produce his knife. "Better leave that rawhide around their wrists until you get them locked up—"

"I reckon I can take care of them," Hillerman said and sliced the cord that locked Tolbert's wrists. Turning to Enright, he cut the leather thongs binding his hands also.

"Fellow tells me you've had them tied up like this for nigh onto two weeks," Hillerman said. "You may be a big important marshal but it ain't right treating human beings that way."

"You've got the wrong idea about them if you think they're human. What they did here in Prescott ought to prove that to you," Rye said coldly. "Now, do what I tell you. Keep them tied up till—"

At that moment Jake Tolbert spun and bent forward. His hand slid into his right boot, came up with a silver-barreled derringer that he had concealed, but, because his wrists were bound together, had not been able to use. Jamming the weapon into Hillerman's side he pulled the trigger and, as

233

the deputy began to fall, jerked the lawman's pistol from its holster. Enright, caught unawares by his partner's actions and hindered by Hillerman's lifeless body, stumbled as he tried to get clear. Regaining his balance, he wheeled to Tolbert.

"Let's run for it!"

Tolbert, covering Rye with the pistol he'd taken from the deputy, nodded, began to back hurriedly toward a wagon on the opposite side of the street. Reaching it, he twisted about, triggered a quick shot at Rye, and dodging in behind the vehicle, began to leg it for the cover of a nearby shed.

Rye, not hit by the hastily fired bullet, drew his weapon. His face was an expressionless mask as he brought the forty-five to shoulder height, leveled it, and waited for the outlaw to reach an open space between the wagon and the small structure. It came a moment later. Jake Tolbert, realizing he was caught in the clear, paused, whirled about, gun again ready to shoot. Rye fired twice in quick succession. The bullets struck the outlaw in the chest before he could use his own gun. Staggering back, he fell to the ground.

"Bone!" the marshal yelled, as smoke drifted away from him. A grim satisfaction, unwanted and unbidden but present never-theless, was coursing through him. "Hold it, or I'll kill you, too!"

Enright came to an abrupt halt and, raising both hands over his head, came about slowly and faced Rye.

"What's going on here? What happened?" Tom asked in a quick rush of words as he came running from his office. He stared disbelievingly at the limp figure of deputy Mason Hillerman sprawled in the dust and, beyond it, that of Jake Tolbert.

"What the hell?" the deputy added, handing a slip of paper to Pearly who was a step behind him. "Mason's dead—so's one of the prisoners—Tolbert—"

Rye, calmly reloading his pistol as the crowd began to move in closer, didn't look up. "Tolbert pulled a derringer out of his boot and shot your man, then tried to get away."

"And you shot him?"

Rye nodded and slid his weapon back into its holster. "Warned Hillerman about cutting their hands loose. Wouldn't listen."

Tom, his pistol out and taking charge of Bone Enright, shook his head. "Town was wanting to hang Tolbert real bad for what he done. One of the reasons the governor sent for you. Figured you'd bring him back alive—"

"Did," Rye said quietly as Pearly came to stand beside him. "Kept him alive for a long time. Went against the grain, but I did it anyway."

Tom frowned. "Good as they say you are with that six-shooter of yours, seems to me you could've just winged him—saved him for hanging, like the governor wanted."

Rye's features hardened. He was thinking of Jake Tolbert, of the brutal crimes the outlaw had committed, of the senseless cruelty he had gloried in—and the disturbing fact that he had almost escaped the hangman's noose that was to be payment for what he had done.

"Yeh, I reckon I could," the lawman said and taking Pearly Joplin by the arm struck off down the street for the bank.

The publishers hope that this Large Print Book has brought you pleasurable reading. Each title is designed to make the text as easy to see as possible. G. K. Hall Large Print Books are available from your library and your local bookstore. Or you can receive information on upcoming and current Large Print Books and order directly from the publisher. Just send your name and address to:

G. K. Hall & Co.
70 Lincoln Street
Boston, Mass. 02111

or call, toll-free:

1-800-343-2806

A note on the text
Large print edition designed by
Fred Welden.
Composed in 18 pt English Times
on an EditWriter 7700
by Cheryl Yodlin of G.K. Hall Corp.